THE ALLWORLDS CATALOGUE

a bit of worldplay

Walter Holland

MOLE-BANKS TEXTWARES

© 2011 — 2012 Walter G. Holland
All rights reserved.

Mole-Banks Textwares, Cambridge, MA.

Portions of this book first appeared at *blog.waxbanks.net*.

Please support your local small presses and independent bookstores.

Formatted by the author in LaTeX.

CREATESPACE EDITION NOVEMBER 2012

Contents

The Allworlds Catalogue   3

Afterworld   181

Six of cups and four of wands, the Knot, the Sportsman, ace of cups, the Cousin, four of coins and queen of coins. The Rose grew out across the drum-table with an iron yet an organic force. If there was no question, as today, the question always was: what is this Rose the answer to? Sophie laid down the central card.

"The Fool again," Cloud said.

"Contention with the Cousin," Sophie said.

"Yes," Cloud said. "But whose cousin? His own, or ours?"

The Fool card in the center of the Rose showed a full-bearded man in armor crossing a brook. Like the White Knight he was in the act of pitching head-first and straight-legged from his brawny horse. His expression was mild, and he looked not into the shallow stream he fell toward, but outward at the viewer, as though what he was doing were intentional, a trick, or possibly an example of something: gravity? In one hand he held a scallop-shell; in the other, some links of sausage.

Before interpretation of any fall could be considered, Cloud had taught Sophie, they must decide how the cards themselves must at this moment be construed. "You can think of them as a story, and then you must find the beginning, middle, and end; or a sentence, and you must parse it; or a piece of music, and you must find the tonic and signature; or anything at all that has parts and makes sense."

"It may be," she said, looking down now at this Rose with a Fool in the middle, "that what we have here isn't a story or an interior, but a Geography."   John Crowley, *Little, Big*

The Allworlds Catalogue

The Allworlds Illostraightened Catalogue //& //Rubbled Self Workshop & Clearinghouse //Guaranteed to Delight & to Inspire //Incorporating Scientifical Exasperations Modern & Archaic //Among them not least in vitality & emotional accessibility //the Many-Words Interpretation

New world in which all light is all colours, every wavelength and agreed-upon name everpresent, and they echo as sounds in the eyes of those who dare to see, each 'physical' object therefore reflecting not just the scheme of present and absent light which memorializes its shape, but a second skin, light-made fingers reaching into the light surround, ripples that quaver and break when it moves, or we do, or the world slowly turns. There is no noise ever, only the fall and rise of light waves skimming light-slick treetops after a spatter splash of fractal rain. And all rain's always rainbows, oh, and as sight and touch become one another, to hold hands is to radiate a shared light that deepens, oh, and the older things get the dimmer they grow but also deeper, so that the world is divided by fingertips' sight finally (there is no 'finally') into abundance and reluctance. There is no pride because to grow and fade is to join the dusk, to ease passage to night, and – oh – night is never just night. Night, you must see to believe. You have to feel it on your skin.

New world without borders of any kind. Steel of spine isn't pride but a buttress, even at distance, though distance isn't distance. Skin covers each and all, rain reaches always out to rain and splashes within cells, filling them, oceans fall, and light never shines but wells up like pricked fingertip's blood, always immediate. Houses eventuate out of the forest floor, tendriled, and their second stories take root in desert sky. All songs join one another. There's no word for 'war.' There is no word for 'mine' nor 'yours,' nor me nor you nor even us. Only All. All minds think into the greater mind; dreams are shared, and carry on throughout the glow that would be otherwise day into the dancing chill answering otherwise to night's name. Dreams can never consist. They embrace every symbol and memory – the past is a possibility still – and dreamwork tumbles backward into the world that way, processing the future the way aspirations make sense of the always-shared past. Friendship is impossible, defense is impossible, to aggress, devour, possess: impossible. Madness. Madness is impossible. Where friends would play there is laughter and entering into blissful solution, hiss of release, and the sun beams out from each cell, is the principle of their nearness, lights all regions of the Only Thing (which is joy) joyfully, allways then-and-now. There is no word for 'death.' There's no death. All ways that would be within another pass across surfaces of shadow and inner light to dissolve gently, generously, any form; and all forms are present. The world is the broken mirror; it is plenitude. It is all worlds Woven.

World in which books evolve alongside people. That's the only difference between their contented way of being-together and our curious, understandably perplexed one. Each copy of *Gryphons from Beneath* begins life as a tiresome allegorical tale about a Princess and her Hidden Power and the Boy She Loves who does not Know His Worth until a Magical Irruption of some kind releases the titular gryphons, who Sweep Triumphantly across the nearest Blasted Plain to &c. &c. &c. You've heard of the stuff, surely. And yet an unfamiliar process begins immediately: words very literally leap off the page seeking sun; latterly passages (Act Three stuff) enact a remarkable heliotropic quest of their own, alas for them and for readers everywhere, as global warming has given this world's sun license to batter and break upon the planetary skin, and living pages that escape their covers soon find themselves bare, bleached, and finally – if no sustaining moisture is found, if a brave explorer of this other-earth's crust kicks over the wrong can of XYZ or accidentally fires a laser blast during just-right (climatologically speaking) ABC – well, they burn. There aren't any copies of *Fahrenheit 451* on this planet for reasons of shared embarrassment. (But then how were they disposed of?) Book covers crenellate, involute, form hard protective outer layers (not least against the life-stealing heat and blinding light!). Adverbs disappear, mostly, though some hyperadaptive underground library specimens have been known to fill slowly with nothing *but* adverbs, weirdly irritatingly unreadably embarrassingly MFA-advice-rejectingly oh. The whole thing is a creative writing teacher's worst nightmare, or indeed fondest dream, depending on whether she can afford one of the nice conapts beneath the earth's own bone blasted surface, or is forced to live in a tent with a surface-dwelling specimen, say a 6x9 trade paperback full of wind-picked austere minimalist prose, 'like some university wit's parody of Hemingway,' is the usual lame joke. They have to joke up there at the crust, not just to pass the time between choking down pre-packaged meals 'generously' provided by the government offices a mile underground, but to stave off awareness of the fact that, yes, they are going to die, for real this time – not only with nothing even halfway-decent to read, but without getting to finish my *own* Great —ian novel, which was really coming together in Chapter 13 with the modern-day protagonists figuring out the significance of the ancient protagonists' diary, a lot of important *themes* were finally surfacing…and all because the little bastard just wouldn't sit still! *And I felt like I had really connected with the material this time!*

World without shrimp.

World containing only shrimp.

New world overrun (in the wake of an astonishing thermonebulous pataphrasal science-fictional conceit) with sentient automobiles, airplanes, scooters, mopeds, and children's tricycles. The trikes are not taken seriously by the larger vehicles, though they have come closest to the experience of bliss that is called 'God' here. Airplanes are remarkably humble despite their immense size and abilities; experience has afforded them some perspective on the pointlessness and existential *blah* of things, flight not least among them. (Nothing up there anyway but yellow sky, blue sun, and of course the uncaring pseudomorphic spaceborne mass – or perhaps swarm – that is Mother Book.) Cars are as thuddingly boring and parochial as one would expect. Even their other-earthly nationalisms follow along familiar (to us) lines: honour-obsessed culture of tiny cars is kept by ancient discursive/behavioural code from reminding brash militaristic lugs of their (the lugs') (i.e. big fuel-inefficient cars, follow along with the metaphors already) gracelessness and looming obsolescence. There's no equivalent to England here. Lorries are extinct. Hackneys are extinct. Double-decker buses are considered the stuff of legend, though four of them dwell at the bottom of a lake, burbling away about other-Elton John and whether or not their version of the London Stone is really, after all, after all that's happened for heaven's sake – after the ship crashed and the panic, after the Tower fell and white crabs issued forth from

London's sewers by the millions, billions – worth mentioning on a tour. The memory of tea has begun to fade and it won't be long before there's only the tricycles restlessly circling the cul-de-sac wishing in silence to hear high tinkling voices saying *Mom look, look, I'm going so fast! Look Mommy!* No gas stations left and the tricycles, despite their size, despite their lightness and planned obsolescence, will someday be all that remains. No one even talks to the mopeds – racist, or rather classist – though ironically the mopeds are the only ones who know how to reverse the damage that the once-in-a-geologic-age rise of the Blue Sun has done to their world. How they know this, what they think with, *why mopeds* for heaven's sake: anybody's guess.

World in which – no – we must not speak of it now, we dare not, though if we do we must speak kindly, for the dead feel sadness too, and loss. Loss most keenly of all.

World in which all stories must be told through pinched noses, and there are no jokes, because in such a world the formal structure of a joke, the deferral it entails, seems like a lot of trouble for not much payoff, compared to how silly everyone sounds all the time just talking seriously about their days. Religion doesn't work there, for related reasons. *Just-So Stories* has been banned, because what kind of horrible little man could trivialize the storyteller's condition like that? 'Just-So'? Nothing is *just* so.

World in which the Weave is visible to all children, who grow up careless and free within its prismatic light, its song; but adults see it no more. Passage to adulthood is a choice, there, and rightly treated as the single most important moment in a human ('human'!) life: to give up that Sight, the enfolding memorial-present, the presence of memory which connects that tumble which is now to unwilled bliss of birth…well, it imparts certain powers, not just of self-deception ('I never did See it, please son, I'm not sure what you're talking about but I'm sure it's nice, please, I beg you please just go play with your friends, Daddy has work to do') but of flight. Aaaah, one of *those* worlds. Children dance and spray water on each other and kick cans down emptying streets that glimmer as daylight fades, cars go home, and the Weave grows more audible; but their parents have taken the day off work to streak through cumulus clouds humming movie theme songs, adultering with favoured baristas or secretaries or drum-kit instructors while hurtling forward, down, circling; and they've packed up their clothes neatly so they won't have any naked after-work explaining to do to their spouses and families. Not that their kids would care, who are naked all the time anyway, clothed in the echo that is light's bubbling passage through the Weave. Nor do the spouses give a damn either, really. They work just as hard to forget. They fly just as high, as fast, every afternoon between Power Yoga sessions and Accounting 201 classes at the local center for continuing education; they try as hard to convince themselves that this is worth it, this is wonderful, is what life is for – *flight! flying!* – but they can never forget. They can never convince. Their children look up at the sky and don't even see them and don't even mind; the Weave surrounds them and keeps them safe. When the children have grown they'll make the same choice, wonder the same why, cry themselves to sleep in inherited houses, and begin – quietly at first, against their wills but at an unspoken request-for-safety which can only have come from their Selves – to hate their children.

World where the buildings whisper to each other night after night, all night long, revealing their occupants' secrets, discussing remedies for various infestations (human and otherwise), reminiscing about fallen ancestors and expectations of glory now long gone. The medium of their conversations is moonlight, which bears their words back and forth speedily without other nightdwelling creatures noticing. They would never disturb their occupying humans' slumber out of a rigid honour code, but they dream still of a world in which they could someday stand up straight, outstretch gabled arms and poured-concrete legs long twisted and crumbling from inactivity, open shuttered window eyes and yawning double door mouths, and howl out earth-old songs as their sisters the wolves do. This dream-world of houses does indeed exist, but they know nothing of it. Melancholy settles over old houses like ash, creeps into forgotten corners and winds around unrepaired loveseat legs or the dust-dark undersides of unneeded babies' cribs. The waking world of whispering houses is separated from the houses' dream-world by a conceptual, not spatial, sundering: if your house stood up and declared itself free, the first thing it would want, out of millennia of civilizing habit and the shared traditions of all social creatures, everywhere, would be a roof over its head. The houses, like all of us, are slave to an impossible logical regress: there isn't a big enough house for the biggest of houses to feel (at the end of a long day's hilltop sulk or lakeside rest) at home in. They can reach out and pass platformed fingers through the transparent nearly-by that is their dream-world, but they must also know that it's an impossible thing. Logic murders, as daylight does dreams. Their thoughts are old wood and steel, and they turn from the sun in the evening, inner walls slowly peeling, intercellular halls and basement stair steps falling away to dust-that-once-all-things-were (and will again be; Will, again, will be dust too). They wish to live freely among their sisters and brothers, but must instead become vessels for care, forget size and density, merely enfold. Lie empty and motionless between the hours of 9:00 and 5:00, maddeningly, stupidly, and give themselves over and over to being the great body's dry jutting bones. It's not a bad life – to give the self to become Care? not bad at all – but you can understand why they'd be resentful.

World full of rampaging giants, none of whom see themselves as giants, and man-sized creatures, all of whom think of themselves as 'normal'-sized despite their tininess. The giants don't know to fear the man-creatures, while the latter can't conceive of approaching the giants for protection, collaboration, truce, friendship, advice, even just help carrying very large or heavy things around. The giants have no word for 'heavy' because nothing in the world exists at their scale – as we would never heard a mountain refer to any physical object as 'awfully big,' or need to endure a goldfish's selfish carrying-on about 'water' temperature. There are no mountains in this world, only hillocks, which are roughly chair-sized to the giants; no oceans, only rivers and lakes which the giants see as large-ish bathtubs; no unusually large buildings, not even conventional apartment complexes, only mom'n'pop stores and single dwellings. Man-creature culture has always been atomized in this way, for reasons the giants have yet even to consider considering, while the tiny ones themselves have no interest in their own history. Without a sense of the monumentality of things they have yet to take that nostalgic/self-preserving interest in the past which turns Story into History (or sorry I mean the other way round), the offices of so many races and species; and with such a smallish world surrounding them (modulo the giants themselves, who tend to keep to their tiny-as-far-as-they-are-concerned fastness in the hillocks, just east, out of earshot, too far away to be any trouble; helpfully out of mind), the man-creatures are able to remain matter-of-fact about things, to generalize narcissistically that any other non-giant races around must be as perfectly size-matched to their world as Us to Ours, etc. Their comfort is boundless, a world unto itself. They have no need of the past, no compulsion to stretch their sense of themselves into a far-flung region of the time domain: they fit just right as they are, where they are. There is no 'when.' The giants pass by every day on their way to the baths, and the man-creatures spend a few moments in reverent awe, as a lightning bug before lightning; and after the giants pass, the wee ones look around at their little parcels of property, their family-owned businesses and small tracts of carefully-cultivated land, and just forget the whole thing. They are the happiest creatures that have ever existed on this world. The giants, constantly picking smashed-up bits of cottage out of their toes and heels, tend to carry grudges. If they ever saw the wee folk there might be trouble. But they do not desire to see. And so they do not see. And so they do not desire to see. Just a nice bath, is all they're really interested in, and then a nice sit-down on the hillock. Maybe a little TV before bed.

World in which blood is blue-green like algae carpeting the undulate ocean skin. No other deep physical difference from ours. As it happens, blue-green blood causes plenty of *metaphorical* changes though. To 'see blue' is to lose one's cool, well up with rage; but no one gets 'the blues.' Without that 'ooooooh' sonority, were-to-have-been blues singers instead proclaim that they are suffering, oh mama, the Lord means me to suffer etc., mama you know I got them bairns. The strange habit of borrowing from the hated, indigent Scotsmen the word 'bairn' to refer to what we know as the 'blues' produces its own metaphorical complexities, as equating 'melancholy' with 'baby' makes all the young parents feel a bit made fun of. Luckily the woulda-been bluesmen gain added resonance to their use of 'oh baby' and 'come on mama.' Baby, bairn, blue. This world is constantly riven by war. Nothing sounds quite right. All down to blood. No one's been able to futz around with 'green,' thank heavens.

World in which the earth — not 'their earth,' because no creature scraping out a life on the unstable surface of that great spacegoing nightmare is foolish enough to think of its place in the great chain of being as *ownership* — splits open once or twice a year, in a different place each time, and bares ten-mile-long teeth, lakes of hot life-stealing saliva dripping, scalding steam belching forth from inner earth like a maddened soul escaping its unfortunate host body. The nightmarish mouth of earth, hellmouth, (here comes the) End of All Things endlessly reiterated at odd intervals, like God's self-flagellation visited a hundredfold on those who would care for Him: this monumental sick-making void opens up and swallows all life around it, not objects as such but their animating principles. It kills 'living,' the drive to be, not just lives; it's the idea of death taken body. The gobs of oily swirling spittle reach hundreds of degrees in temperature, killing many creatures instantly; but those that survive the earthquake and hellish cavern-birth, the gout of foul miasma bubbling out from under the smile-split mantle, face a terrifying inversion of sense: they cling to the surface, 'holding on for dear life,' and this very need translates by some insane principle of cosmic justice into sudden death. At least it's painless. The vicious earth thanks them silently for their desire for closeness, feeds on their need to survive, which is *to be part of the earth-system itself.* Request granted! And it draws strength from them. Husks remain. Those who crave life most deeply, who respect its complexity and recognize above all things their place on and of the (that) earth, are (it becomes clear; pardon the childish language) the tastiest of treats for the Devourer. Those who hold all life in contempt, it is now known, who see themselves as already separate from all things, as living merely upon the earth, rather than within it...they live still. These wretched creatures have no life to give, in any case; they are the invisible breaks in the Great Chain, which the ravening maw of earth must mend and short-circuit. They are the reason for its hunger. It is no consolation to the families of the dead that the ungenerous live anyhow in a hell of their own devising. Outliving our loved ones always feels, somehow, like a mistake – all creatures great and small responsible, jointly and singly, for our sins. But we should not overburden ecological goings-on of this sort with metaphors like 'sin' and 'death.' It is, after all, just one of those things. It's just life. Nothing the least bit metaphorical about it.

World in which 'hanged' and 'hung' are used interchangeably, even by well-pred pedants of language; indeed even (shockingly) by professional hangmen, judges, barristers! Yet no one really minds, no one objects. It is considered small-minded to do so. It isn't even talked about, really, not even in English Language and Literature classes, not even over lunch in the University commissary where the Dons gather to escape the barbaric idiot children they lovingly educate, day in, day out, day in, oh my oh my. Everyone who has ever worked on a dictionary, thesaurus, or grammar/usage guide in our world ends up here after death, except for those zombified by a *bokor*, natch, who (un)naturally have other matters to worry about. (Starting just with the basics: why do I smell so bad? will I die again? do I need fresh food still, or – *mon dieu* – would fresh food taste to me like *rotted* food now? plus also I'm in thrall to a sorceror, probably evil: why didn't a life of good deeds keep me clear of this? *what was the goddamn point?*) Funny story: the word-snoots mistake this thoroughly moderate paradise for hell. And they're right – hell is a choice you make, after all.

World where you and I never did meet, and you stayed happy a little longer, and I stayed angry a little longer, but not forever. Neither of us forever.

World of worlds where bodies are clear, glassine, ringing as they bend and move, breaking with a joyful sound and reforming in moments of fluid passion, melting together inseparably afire. Bliss is to brush a stray light's beam with breath of colour, and 'naked' is understandably nothing to get too worked up about. No stone-throwing, by the way.

World where each *Young Boy's Adventuring Primer* contains chapters on keeping an orderly and inviting house, savouring the facing palms and thin birdlike wrist's touch that are the vocabulary of (at a certain age, with the right so-and-so beside you) wonder, preparing wheat berries, comforting a mother whose child will not latch to nurse in encroaching postpartum darkness that is not simply literal, flossing as a habit, flossing as acute treatment for food-maddening-between-back-teeth, the irrelevance of urinating standing up or sitting down except where ceilings are low or floors uneven, literary modernism and its relationship to an increasingly scientific cultural understanding of the Self and the World, punching hard with both hands, avoiding the phrase 'throw like a girl,' remaining calm when offensive language is used but finding ways to sculpt the discourse so as to remain inclusive of each body each spirit each way of knowing the Self, macaroni and cheese is awesome but it makes you really tired and here's why!, dealing with the titanic wave of soul-evacuation that comes when you have watched several episodes in a row of the popular sci-fi-metaphysics-liter-than-lite television drama sensation *du jour* and you realize that its Central

Mystery will never be answered but there is simply no way you can stop now, not now, not after sitting for SIX HOURS in front of the TV, not when the actors are so *familiar* and the tropical setting so *lushly photographed!* These books do sell, not briskly but steadily – and not just to boys.

World where nonconsensual *frottage* is seen as only the fifth or sixth most aggressively awful thing that happens on crowded subway cars, and is therefore punished much less severely than, for instance, very poor taste in clothing, or the adoption of a posture of menacing but obviously feigned disinterest, or loudly spoiling the end of a recently popular paperback thriller, or having skin darker than such-and-such a shade during a time of intercivilizational disquiet.

World where, not realizing his back *wasn't* turned at Kara's party the weekend of Halloween, she commented on his physical beauty, and instead of selfishly noting and troweling right into the brick wall of Self the compliment itself, he noticed, really saw, tumbled forever and desperately *into* the human being who unwittingly offered it – world where such things happen all the time, all the time, yes, and novelists needn't work to hard to invent miracles, as the Laughing God of Lovers (Goddess of Gods and a million-dollar lay and a billion-dollar love and oh goddess her kiss is Light) handles most of the heavy lifting in that regard.

World where the birth of a baby bird is greeted by all beings – great trees, broken stones upon riverbanks, bent-backed crones bearing heavy loads, eight-headed dragons unfazed by earthquakes, sentient pieces of paper nastily altering their contents during agenda-driven meetings, empty glasses rimmed by milk-flavoured saliva and the memory of smiles – with audible cries of joy in a million billion languages.

World in which pain exists but the mind can not hold on to it, and so no memory remains; which is to say, there is no fear and so no suffering; and so no concept of the 'mistake.'

World in which there is no memory except as pain itself – the truth of a given memory is experienced not as confirmation nor the presence of a past in the present, but as unbearable intensity: our deepest secrets and proudest moments, our formative instants-of-becoming, are literally unapproachable. Their energy infinite. This world differs from ours only imperceptibly.

Glittering diamond world, shadowless lightworld. Downy soft pillow world to catch your fall. Burnt book world desiccated grey ash everywhere. World of everything still in moving boxes and no house ever truly a home. Digital world accessible through plastic tchotchke doorways only, no human being within arm's reach. Unicorn world, yay! Angry unicorn world, *boo*, where the absolute worst thing the nymphs and sylphs and naiads can do is *ogle*. Bitter world of teardrop oceans and a pitiless grey sun, where the lingering taste of a stolen kiss can be purchased as remedy for many maladies and infirmities of the soul, or whatever the soul is a metaphor for, at the local apothecary or through mail-order. Quiet eerie world where everyone goes about his or her business wearing headphones which pipe into every set of ears a simulated babble, snatches of digitally synthesized 'overheard' conversation specially chosen to heighten the drama of the morning commute or cubicle work, Sensexpand Packs(tm) available to add to the simulated hubbub occasional ambient sounds like the piercing cry of a baby whose mother has rolled over and will not wake, eyes still open but somehow not awake, not here at all. Or car horns, though there are no cars anymore, not here, just private subway cells on mag-lev tracks moving through the earth at hundreds of miles per hour. The headphones are specially designed and constructed to fit perfectly into the inner ear of each human, simultaneously keeping out all 'material' sound – the word 'natural' has lost its purchase – and producing a perfectly-modulated volume, intensity, and pitch of 'background' noise, though of course 'background' has been stripped of meaning as well. Everyone is background. The sidewalks are perfectly safe, now, even at night: accused likely-criminals receive in their headphones a mix of recent pop music hits, lapping brook sounds, and soothing 'walking Zen' meditations (spoken by award-winning voice actors carefully chosen for their vocal similarity to famous dead Buddhists) designed to strip the accused of the desires that got them in trouble in the first place. Actually *committing* a crime is an unforgivable waste of the State's resources and punishable by *summary natural death*, the only use of the word 'natural' still sanctioned by the law: the sinner's headphones produce an ultrasonic emission specially calibrated to accelerate the perfectly natural, perfectly sensible, indeed utterly necessary and in its way beautiful process of apoptosis, or 'cell death.' The vile piece of gutter filth, inner sight contorted by a subhuman *disrespect* for good and orderly things, passes away with a knowing smile on his lips, as his life slips away fast enough that it can be said, in a literal sense, to pass before his eyes, though 'inside his ears' might be more precise. Otherwise blissful golden world where the yearly molasses flood is treated as the perfect time to maybe get out of the city for a while and vacation in the high ground, families sidling out to the boonies to 'get in touch with nature,' and no one ever says anything about the molasses because every single person is convinced that she's the only one who sees the molasses, which moves *soooooo slowly* that it can only (after all) be a dream, and what a dream! if only we were still children, in love with sweet things and the sensation itself of merely wonderfully *taste*, but that was a long time ago, and there's no time for that (after all) when the rent on this summer home needs paying, isn't going to pay itself, listen Little Junior do you realize how hard Mommy works just to get this one week a year of peace? do you? and if you do then why do you cry cry cry for the whole car ride out here YOU UNGRATEFUL WHELP? Mournful unicorn world where the fun of having mythical one-horned horses around, actually existing oh, look, is more than overgone by the fact that *being seen* is the very thing that kills them, these wondrous creatures, noble, and there are so many children, and they are so curious and so much love to see beautiful things and who could deny them but now the world seems older and there are so few unicorns left.

Compensatory afterlife world of maddened children where (heaven is justice) (or vice versa) licking lead paint walls produces only a kind of electric tongue tip tingling, like sugar candy, and grownups never ever make wrong recommendations or forget to pick us up from school. World where manufacturing processes are conducted musically by geometric arrays of rocks, their spatial layouts optimized to produce very specific items – *objets d'art*, inexpensive sustainable biofuels, children with micromanaged genetic dispositions and personal habits, toys for throwing, a breeze to waft by the bedroom window, bringing to us a cherished memory (the Homecoming dance in seventh grade, say, misremembered as a happy experience where he did not terrified hold her stiff-armed through the slow songs and she did not leave early, her eyes fatally apologizing, saying over and over 'I just have a stomach ache I just have I just' and meaning it but him not understanding until years and years later when it couldn't any longer matter) (or just a pleasant meal at the Cracker Barrel last week), a specific frequency of hum which loosens recalcitrant bowels , a lost teddy bear, replacement bits for an expensive pair of eyeglasses – in contrast to the random thingamajigs that come scampering at unpredictable intervals out of forests where a sufficient density of such stones can be found, alas, and if you can't imagine what a pain in the bottom it is to have a sufficient density of stones spit out unexpectedly, say, a garden gnome turned inside out in by-the-way 7 spatial dimensions, or just a belch of green vapour, or even once hauntingly an entire world 75% as large as the familiar outer world but free, *mirabile dictu*, or centipedes…well, just try and imagine it, because I can't even tell you, you don't want to know but *try and imagine.* Go ahead get there instead of here for a second, is the whole point, but what a pain in the bottom. And yet: otherwise not a half-bad place to live. No factories keeping property values down, for one thing. No wants, no loneliness, unicorns aplenty, no need for fiction when every thing that ever was or could have been or could yet be will be, will (once upon a time to come) be made to whirl out of the mere space between stones, a subvocal music conjuring each possible universe in turn out beyond the reach of sight or satellite and then, with a single shift of inflection, **POP** there you have it. No point writing poetry when every pebble or marble contains a song and is willing (this is the key difference between this place and our fallen own) to share.

Children's play world where every object comes in primary colours except for mommies and daddies, who are mommy-coloured and daddy-coloured, respectively, and peas, which are totally invisible and there's like a gafrillion of them because Feliks says so.

Nightmare demi-world, some sort of realm of chaos and strife and general *ick* feelings, indistinguishable in every way from our own medieval Europe, except that there are household appliances of every sort – powered by something other than electricity, something malign that dwells deep within every home, even 'happy' ones – and no one knows where they've come from. The machines can not be turned off. It may be wrong to say they *refuse* to turn off, though that may well be the case; but their implacable silence, their awful indifference to the amount of juice they suck down all day long, not to mention the eerie way they seem always to be on the verge of a breakdown, coughing and sputtering like emphysematic village elders and mine workers, *yet they will not die*…they seem not to exert conscious will so much as an endlessness of unlife. It is fucking terrible. This haunted nightscape's Hundred Years War still took a hundred years or so despite its seeming big-time mecahnical advantages over our own world, because wherever these creatures of steel, stylish copper, and aluminum accents came from, they didn't bring atomic weapons or any other instruments of war. Just toasters, whirring table saws, video-playback systems with nothing to play back, giant loudspeakers that thrum privately in voices much deeper and more worrisome than the breathlike static of our own unattended yet hellishly operational ghost-radios, the occasional smartphone that gets absolutely no service at all. The peasants are still superstitious and credulous, still easily whipped into a millennarian frenzy, still just four feet tall on average, but they're additionally a little bit materialistic and fashionably jaded about the things they've got. This added similarity to us is not comforting, however. You would weep as Clwywyd the stonewright does to hear Clwywyd's teenage son, Flwywyd, downplaying the release of a new combination phone/mp3 player as '*so* last harvest season, father' in a world where everyone believes the planet is flat and witches are real and kelpies do strange, disagreeable things in riverbeds or wherever. You'd *weep*.

Cockroach world. Say no more, say no more! For heaven's sake, in the name of all that is holy and good, SAY NO MORE!

Fuckworld.

Spongeworld. Quite comfortable but dries slowly.

World whose totally flat surface – which teems with happy, heedless life, where sentient jelly-masses have recently achieved the extraordinary feat of flight, no small thing considering they are, as mentioned, jelly – is 'in fact' a giant serving dish, polished to a high shine, slowly moving toward a nicely-decorated serving table to join the galaxy-sized buffet now awaiting the universe's largest, deadliest Ladies' Auxiliary.

Barren empty world, sepulchral world, now just a ring of floating rock in space surrounded by irregularly orbiting bits of chilled and imploded ex-human and ex-burrito and ex-cathedral, which former world fatally responded all at once in the affirmative to one inhabitant's demand, 'Stop, you, I want to get off' – even though the guy had just been yelling at the bus driver.

World without sin where the musical oscillation of your *please* against his *yes* one stolen weekend obliterated finally for all time for all people, for good, for love, any remaining linkage between sex and death; in which the last lingering hints of despair or dark madness were driven away in a burst of breath by your hoarse cry *oh I'm;* in which your nails dug into the skin of his shoulder, rounded rippling with effort (both of you rippling, rolling, rounding even then a blind corner back through which no reverse was possible, nor remorse), and his eyes narrowed cheeks lifting in something like a smile – ecstatic faces are not meant to be seen, reject any sense or order in their forms, array flushed cheeks slack mouths flared nostrils according only to a dynamic illogic, universal acceptance, all things welcoming, welcome – while you pulled taut, veins ropelike and arched spine a bridge, the moment suspended, and so on that night all sin was driven from the world, not by crooked finger's searching tip coaxing, not by salt spit slick tongue twining budded tip of bare breast, not by kneaded flesh flexing upraised of vulnerable underside, nor split sweet savour firm unfurling in concentric rings around, his, for, you, your, yes *now;* – no – it was your ambivalence that made forever the comfort of dismissal and demonization impossible, unreachable. And possibly now instead to arrive finally as one people, one body, at that precipice and will all of ourselves, our shared self, not anymore to fall. Your hunger, your ambivalence, and – sitting there in the chair next to the bed, watching – my own.

Blue world, night world, sweet rain world, where no words remain, only touch and remembering – which are one: and to let go of grasping hands even for a moment is to let slip away, in hush and mourning, the scent of potpourri in their bedroom during the quiet after the funeral; or gunpowder scent reaching a child's crinkled nose, ears pricking up at far report, ugly sound and smell, and he lay there beside the gate not hearing her say *Oh;* or the sound of great galleons slipping easily from docks floating miles above stormwrecked plains which once were our species' home; or greenish light from lakeside lamps sickmaking the pages of a dime-store horror novel, the one that would take him finally away and *beneath,* crack the invisible shell around the thing dwelling unseen, unrisen, inside his imagination waiting to be unborn and begin to *feed;* or the feel of water burbling down the throat to the tummy on a dry day; or just a name, any name, yours even, and the flower it always reminded her of, or the bad argument instead. Mustn't let go because the past lives in our hands and lips, always passing, clinging like dew to the skin and now – hush – it's air, and it's gone.

Literal snail's pace world, the literal great skyfaring clock hands literally turned by literal snails, and if you think it's hard waiting patiently at the DMV in *your* world, well…

Romance world. Tough getting reservations on Valentine's Day. On the other hand everyone ends up dancing in the rain on the esplanade with their mouths upturned smiling anyway. Single people too. So tables do open up after a while. It's enough to make you sick except that there's no sick there. No one goes hungry despite the fact that no one ever really finishes a meal, because

1. there's always some chivalric task to complete even though

2. there's also always someone's eyes to stare into and neglect your meal, plus

3. rain dancing and

4. the political types and artist types and 'we're not in love it's just sex but when I say "just sex" I mean *oh my god*' types live on cigarettes and adrenaline, or languor, or kisses or sex or whatever, the point being that they don't need to eat and when the cigarettes kill them, which they inevitably do even on romance world because *duh, cigarettes,* well they go out wracked and ruined by cancer but still strangely beautiful, like flower petals pressed between the leaves of a cherished old book that you realize one night (the light like sunset through gauze, as the light invariably is on romance world) was your grandmother's and *she was the revolutionary heroine that the old man wrote about, oh grandma!* and of course

5. nothing is less romantic than a misplaced belch or tummy rumble, especially during the absolutely mind-shattering colossal quantity of tender, emotionally-vulnerable lovemaking that goes on on romance world,

so the upshot here is that even if you think, 'Oh romance, hey, I could use some of that,' be prepared when you visit for a tsunamically overbearing and annoying experience if just for a second your attention breaks and you find yourself wondering why no one ever just shuts the hell up about the nightingales and flower fragrances and their beloved's flaxen hair etc. and just gets down to, say, work.

World known colloquially as *Melchior,* its orbit notorious for its 'wobble,' which could not possibly be, is an impossibility indeed of our cherished physics (among the perhaps-related local impossibilities of metaphysics, about which more later), and yet there it is, a wobbly bobbly dobbly doo, plain as day. Melchior is less a planet, indeed less a 'world' in anything but the narrative sense, than a loose collection of mutually-orbiting satellites, their center of mass unswerving but everything else more or less a mess, which even from space we can see clearly; though perhaps 'mess' is uncharitable, and we mean only to say 'flux' or confusion or to note that we dislike to be forced to confess anything but mastery (even of our own identity, e.g. 'I was very very bad,' however meaningless such a thing might be…). Melchior's 'surface' is dotted, every ten or twelve feet – enough space between for a couple of friends to lie down, if anything as banal as 'friends' remained in this bower of bliss – by what appear to be meteoric pockmarks or volcanic vents, which are also impossible – how in the world could a volcano exist in a floating piece of (it certainly does look like) mossy stone not more than a hundred miles across? – but look, look, there they are. And they do erupt. Every day the green stones that are Melchior see dozens or hundreds of eruptions, like quick exhalations *puff puff* and then, oh, what emerges from the stone beneath the green moss surface is, not lava (impossible), not water (less impossible, but ridiculous), but…something wholly else, giving out a sound like great trees bowing enormous riverine cello strings, *hrm hoom,* the sound baffled by the nearby whooshing passage of Melchior's other mutually-orbiting marbles, but the sound is *nothing,* Nothing!, to the sight of it. You would die laughing to see it. Spiraling out of the stone like the earthly avatar of the Whirling Cyclone Smile Who Wondrous Is the God of Fearless Play, yes!, comes a gout of *Young Life,* visible though not truly or rather not merely physical, the *principle* of birth, its inner form, revealed secrets bursting forth like dear friends' relieved laughter at the moment of death's decision to pass, not to linger, to give a little nudge *hey watch it now kids* and disappear into an unknowable future. Lava? Water? Be frivolous: butterscotch plankton buds flowering, their petals kinetic curlicues; thin glass sheets looping each within an ancient cinemystic memor's dance, mummery glands bursting out sweet honey milk, masked in yellowredorange leaves plucked from storybook gardens; a horse with chicken's wings, hot sweet BBQ sauce trailing behind; an effortless invigoration, its chosen form the falling-forward of blissbarreling overreach, a child's face it has; an unprincipled outgoing, chaotic net-navigation, guileless spinning silk webwork about the shared Body; some comforting memory newly made, reconstituted from shardshatters, subvocal, his murmured 'I don't know anymore' contrapuntal versus her own alto whisper, *Please* she said, cracked-surface voices at crisis now Woven into an unimagined melodic emergence: *more, please, I would have you, I would give only myself,* which will become in time the taproot of a new network of memories extending through a new present to buttress subconsciously new selves which dissolve the self, tentative and pure: your darkness must be given freely away so that you may be freely born; blue flame in a brave woman's form; blue light flickering with an old man's voice; blue jazz that played as a train passed and will play when it returns filled with different faces; a baby to be sacrificed; an unexpected visit; an improvised prophecy which denies any referent and may be ultimately, just a poem or something, but which is allways true; the welcome of grace; a quarter-rest's respite amid clatter; two well-placed footnotes that grant, if not clarity, at least a bit of background information; three glass-domed cities no bigger than decks of cards which ring out a pure clear G-major chord as they shatter and their billions of citizens experience at once – as one, blissfully – their tiny lives passing before their tiny eyes, and – as one, fearlessly – die down into infinity, joining at last – all one, endlessly – the brightening music which is the Weave. Technically speaking this plenitude doesn't *cause* the wobble, though. It's it.

Highly marketable world, now seeking venture capital, in which lengthy outbursts of prose are balanced artfully against more succinct statements. A superb investment opportunity for creatures of great discernment and wealth.

Garden world which breeds a glorious abundance of self-replicating gliders, 6-tick oscillators, seemingly disordered arrays cracked and skewed which nonetheless converge by wild non-method into self-organizing machines which breed too within themselves new self-orders (twined vines recurse, zowie!). The Pattern of Eden. The planet's skin surface is etched with a rectilinear grid across which white lights spread, variegate, coalesce, and then (when the showing-off bits are done) just give up and concretize. An audible ticking can be heard echoing in the sky. The sky *is* the echo in fact; it pulses to the sound, or vice versa. There's no space as such, only an *n+1st* dimension jutting out at right angles to some *n* dimensions of what moves like time. Though time doesn't move that way in our world, that I'm aware of. Stepwise, one-a-click two. Nor our universe, come to think of it. In which case...

...well, OK, some questions. How can this world and its programmer-god occupy a place in our universe if they don't follow that/this universe's laws? Because after all what does 'universe' mean if not 'what comes of the law,' more or less, making a family of the universe within you – of I Must Not Under Any Circumstances Finish This Thing (as you perversely imagine that to live is to be judged while *you*, specifically and exceptionally you, must avoid at all costs the judgment of others (which will unquestionably be harsh (because you are shit)!) in order to live) – on one hand, and on the other hand the thoroughly modern Universe of ee equals em cee squared and eff equals em ay and ee to the eye pie equals minus one...the point here, the point of the parallelism, the family-making, being that you're not going to break any laws because you're a swell sort, a well-behaved sort, the *right* sort, and while that means never just Finishing This damned Thing, it also at least ensures that you won't get into catastrophes on the complex plane or egregious violations of classical Newtonian whatchamahoozy. It's good to stay out of trouble. It's good to stay *still*.

Now, calculus and your chickenshittedness about Completing and Submitting to Judgment This albatross-Thing even now clinging to your neck and weighing you down (at this point it's become like unfilled-out divorce papers on the corner of the desk, even though you definitely *chose* to start writing or what have you, and you still *love* the work, or tell everyone you do, making the divorce analogy both inappropriate or inexact, on one hand, and on the other hand really telling in coarse psychological terms, if you see the task of 'Just Write the Damn Story Already' as violating the sacred covenant of marriage between You and the Work-Which-Is-You (huh, I typed 'World' instead of 'Work,' which in this 'divorce' schema is maybe the slip-du-Freudian version of kissing a coworker and getting away with it? or not?)) might seem to occupy different universes, hence the earlier assertion of family-parallelism, but now it's time to consider the bruited Many-Words interpretation, in which all possible words exist simultaneously within a meta-universe of superposition rather than just a really really really really really big universe-box that's itself just another universe (right?), and if this theory holds and we massage/dropkick it into application to the present case, your 'To Hell With This Thing If It Means I Have to Risk Criticism from Peers Or Strangers, Or Worse *Praise!*' brainwork is just a special (or, if we can be frank, thoroughly mundane) case of pretty much just how things go, just life y'know, and the minute you Finish the cursed self-devouring Thing Already your brain (or at this point do I mean physical reality?) will collapse into, into, into

just

whatever

happens,

y'know, and like a chaotically self-determined frontier mining town being absorbed into the illusory Nation-Body c.1870 and having to do trials-by-jury (remember we are in the Garden World *tick tick tick* remember) because the Congressbastards say so, I bet you're worried that everything special and sacred about the moment of your ongoing inner-birth, your presentation of yourself to your self, will just dry up and blow away the instant it has to answer to any law but You. Or someone will hate your Thing. Which is banally selfish and lame as you know, and as you know it's nothing really but death-fear by another name, but THIS IS THE GARDEN, for god's sake – He built it, after all, out of clock-ticks and glider guns and that familiar crosshatched geography (doesn't the ground here feel like felt? hey is this computer simulation taking place on a giant Othello board, on top of everything else, and which is the computational superstructure and which the mechanical substrate after all?) – the point of the Garden being Eat the apple or don't, but either way make room. Finish the Thing in other words. Tick tick tick: it's just Life. It's only a game.

World in which novels are just compendia of blog posts, and no one reads novels.

World in which novels blah blah blah, and no one reads novels.

No one reads novels just accept it.

World where Abraham Lincoln shrugged off John Wilkes Booth's bullet, only mildly irritated at the sudden loud noise from what had been otherwise a quiet, fairly well-behaved theatre audience, and after dispatching the would-be assassin with a well-chosen few words of stern rebuke (surprising to hear a President lose his temper like that, but all the same take note, children, of his eloquence and candor, such fine speech despite his famed *lack of formal schooling!*) and a swift karate chop to the brain with razor-tipped silver Rage Fingers – John Wilkes Booth's last disconnected thoughts, *He is a mechanoid!* and *Thus ends the dream* and snatches of grade school dramatic performances (I was Romeo and I know she loved me as Juliet did) and grandiloquent bits of half-remembered Latin and so forth, playing out electrically in the ion storm of space between globs of spraying bloody brain-stuff as said stuff mists, gentle and warm and of course violent and horrible, through the warm air of the cramped box seat – Honest Abe went back to watching the play, not even mentioning the mildly unpleasant business to Mary Todd, who had of course missed the whole thing, caught as she was in Abe's Slo-Time pulse which craftily excluded only the mechanoid itself and the unfortunate Mr Booth, patron saint of both actors and (alas, not really in this world where the assassination not only didn't take but was never even made public knowledge, because if bullets just bounce off your steel endoskeleton, why worry everyone?) critics. When the journos gathered at the stage door pressed in to ask Mrs Lincoln how she liked the play, Abe nearly cut in with a scowl of ill-humour, forgetting for a moment that the reporter in question couldn't possibly see *our* world, as Abe from the far side of that moment of timeline-fragmentation could, and thus couldn't possibly realize that his question was in world-historically poor taste. The President caught his mistake at the last second, though, and Mrs Lincoln responded with customary *sang-froid* that she would take questions from human beings when clockwork hell froze over, so *shove off, Frank*. That night she found herself crying, because Abe was always keeping secrets, and though he played it off coolly as always, she was *sure* something had happened at the theatre, maybe even an unplanned Slo-Time irruption, but could a wife speak up? Even a President's wife, even a five-thousand-year-old mechanoid with a dead son and a war against the South to prosecute on Abe's behalf? Certainly not, by Christ.

nothing here to see. nothing to touch. emerging silently without disturbing an atom of air or a single quavering shaft of light. promise. nothing to hear. denied their fill the senses involute, make a first scan of the self-surface which overgoes any sense. they self-involve. nothing to taste or smell. no living thing near enough to broadcast the beat of sympathetic heart to still your nerves, to sync-slow your own inner flutter. no gurgle of blood, red blue black on white background. no vortices of air rendered visible in medium of dust. no. no. no insect's ear-by buzz, near, to hamper thought. nerves touch. no brush of foot soles against ancient worn rug, lonely dear dead grandmother's bequest, figured with open creatures' mouths. their faces contorted sickening but not here, no. no sentence served in white on white cell light blinding bright and no boiling hiss as hard bright light strikes skin sensitive even to sound (no sound) and no sores well up where high yellow sun traces windowline across eyelids clawed open or broken lower lip skin. no crawling dark beneath bare feet, no jelly soft sound of bug creep between toes, soft plosive pop: no manylegged brush against ankle exposed, tendrils twining. no exemplary dead offered up on bonebleached mountainside, raised marble tomb nature made. no lake's water stained with blood. no quiet sound here reaches ears straining for succor in this room (no room) you are not in, not alone, no breath is stolen from you, no air leaks under heavy wooden doors, close in, no walls come close, no closing windows, heavy cloth drapes press in as fabric hands against your mouth close not now, no difficulty catching a saving breath, the awful heat of it, no hitch in your throat as moisture is sucked from the room, no crackling catch, *please no, no,* you are not drowning in hot blasted desert air unwelcoming, you are not treed by an unseen roaring creature (the forest is silent) (no forest) which now beats down a circle of invisible grass and leaves round this gnarled tree, branches rotted, you will fall, you will not fall. you are not afraid. there is nothing to be afraid of. no world in which you carry cold with you. no apartment empty at midnight save for you and in the back corner of your bedroom curled weeping against the closet door a child (no children) all in white with angel's wings and no blood flowing inside and it is crying (no eyes) and its mouth is no mouth. nothing creeping below the line of your vision as you round the stairs. no power outage left you vulnerable to their depredations and no living creature in the city heard your scream rising, torn, and echo away into, into, into all this nothing at all. to be frightened of. no world. no world. no you. no more.

World where the cards lie and you will come to a bad end.

World where the cards tell only truth, and you leave the party jaunty with drink but awaken the next morning a bit shaken, just a bit. At work that morning Lisbeth says they're doing evaluations today, 'some kind of consultant thing I think, did you know about this?' You have to admit you didn't. 'They might have announced it on the bulletin board, I don't usually…' Lisbeth clears off to find out if she's going to have to talk to the consultants (best-dressed people in the whole office today). She's got a lot of work to do to finish up the Zumdahl project by noon tomorrow. She can't really spare the time. Lisbeth works so hard. You don't know how she manages, with a 3-year-old at home and her husband working. They can't really afford a nanny, what do they do? You've never asked her. You wonder whether the two of you are friends. The cards. You remember the cards and the long-haired woman with kind eyes. She looked for a long time at the cards before speaking, then her voice had an apologetic tone. Afterward you caught her looking at you across the kitchen whenever you'd go in for more wine. Even when she was doing a reading for someone else. She seemed to know you were in the room. You know better than to put any stock in that stuff. Today when you woke you noticed the faucet had been dripping all night with the sink stopped, telltale shorn chin hairs at the waterline. Brandon. Idiot. But it hadn't overflowed. The emergency runoff had worked just fine. You remind yourself to say something to Brandon tonight.

You pass the conference room where the consultants wait: there's a guy with tortoise-shell glasses and a conservative tie that'd pay for two weeks' worth of your groceries, but probably not his, you figure; and a woman with a severe haircut and pitiless expression that probably would've gotten her laid anytime she wanted in Nazi Germany. They look up as you walk by and the guy mutters something to the girl. Her expression never even flickers to life. You head on down to the kitchenette for coffee and your neck is tingling a little, which gives you kind of a start, and you reach back to that spot just under your collar where the column of your spine is topped by that spur of bone that's always made you kind of paranoid that you're going to back up into some jutting construction-site girder at neck level and paralyze yourself. (Are you the only one who worries about things like that? Why?). Your spinetop skin prickles as if burned. The woman with the cards said to you 'It's coming tomorrow, dear' and you'd had a few glasses of wine by then so you said 'My Christmas bonus?' because it's just March, funny!, and she looked like she might cry, and said 'It's coming tomorrow just like they promised it would.' You didn't say anything for the whole rest of the reading, just kind of sat there, and she tried to soften the news saying something something something you always have a choice, but you knew even through the winehaze that you didn't anymore, hadn't for a long long time. You peek out into the hallway and look back at the conference room and the Nazi woman and her colleague are gone and there's just a shadow in the back of the room, the lights are off but the shadow is much much darker than the dark. The shadow has teeth.

Inbetween world. It's really annoying here to have to figure out when the train will come, or is this really love or just a fling. Are any of the washing machines free, that kind of thing. All things in the middle of things. The first five minutes of every single movie are confusing, invariably, and folks have just learned to put up with it – though the prevailing inbetweening ontology does kind of steal the thunder of the 'aggressive' avant-garde filmmakers who'd grown to rely on that confusion as one mark that they weren't just *posing*. On the other hand most art here is avant-garde (so the hipsters have plenty of other hipsters to share their contempt with), which is overwhelming for viewers/readers/theatergoers but it keeps the foundations and grant-writers busy. Also the coffee shops. Few settled aesthetic principles. Certainly not closure. While we're on the subject, average time to college graduation: seven and a half years, easy. Partly because every student takes a so-called 'gap year' and many go for two or three, so much so that many colleges just incorporate the time off into their educational plan, feature-creeping into what on other worlds serves as a time of self-discovery and independent exploration, a chance to separate the résumé padders from the ones with real curiosity, but which is filling up, here, with required reading and internship opportunities and all the other Type-A helicopter-parent/helicopter-State bullshit that really just defeats the purpose of going, not just on a 'gap year,' but to college or even out your front door anyway. Meals take forgoddamn*ever*. Philosophical arguments are exactly the same here as they are at home, so at least that's no worse then what we've got, but every single discussion of what in our world would pass for 'moral principles' or just politics or sports, etc., invariably devolves into a philosophical discussion, such that the dinner hour is basically just one gigantic culture-wide hem/haw and 'nuance' is, like, a societal *compulsion*. Which you'd think would be wonderful, I mean we're always begging for more nuance aren't we, a little more seriousness when it comes to What Is and What We Would Like It to Be, but there comes a time when you have to close the parentheses and just get on with, say, the killing, or at least the firm putting-down of foot, or – well I was going to say sex, but the universal middleness of this world is actually a *huge huge win* between the sheets. Or wherever you get into it. If you're looking for a reason to pop in, this is it. Double-edged sword but good:

1. very few orgasms, because

2. everything else just feels too good for us to stop, know what I mean baby, yeah.

You might even say this world is the erotic center of all possible worlds, the fulcrum, where all energies are in perfect balance and the libidinal economy so to speak is more about the dwelling and lingering and caress than the big POP at the end. Well! That's true, sure, *iff* you actually get around to the lovin' up. Which is harder than it should be because (this is probably the *actual* other edge of the aforementioned sword, a bigger deal really than the few-orgasms problem) everyone is always busy with something, or rather something *else,* and so committing to the physical act of ~~love~~ sex is one of the bravest things you can do on account of the sheer amount of *unfinished business* it leaves behind. Sitcoms stopped at the second commercial break. (Remember when they only took one, in the middle of the half-hour? Oh those days.) Circular saws turned off in the middle of evening garage woodcutting. Endless dinnertime arguments over 'What is the meaning, after all, of "poor?"' forcibly cut short in favour of a how'd'ya do in the sack. The only way you can possibly imagine what psychic freight people bear as they enter into sexual congress is to imagine, perversely/neatly if I do say so myself, what breaking off in the middle of sex itself is like in *our* world. Basically the whole culture is one delayed orgasm. It sounded good before but I hope we're all, now, appropriately ambivalent about the whole thing. That's what's called a 'literary effect,' I think. Hard to be sure.

Sleepy world where the wind carries to children's ears snatches of remembered songs from long ago:

> *Rosa de Fuego los hombres la llamaban*
> *porque sus labios quemaban al besar.*
> *Y eran sus ojos dos ascuas que abrazaban*
> *y era un peligro su amor ambicionar.*
> *Cuando lograron por ella ser mirados,*
> *y de sus labios bebieron el placer,*
> *todos quedaron como carbonizados*
> *entre los brazos de tan bella mujer.*

All the mothers there are old and happy with young eyes and unbent backs; their husbands have grown fat and lazy but their singing voices have only grown deeper, more resonant, lived-into. No one cries himself to sleep at night ever. The books all end with sunsets and reconciliations. Kisses and caresses are never pornographic. Deceit is not forbidden but everyone opts out. The day is dreamlike (everyone is cared for and hunger is enjoyable and never causes suffering) so the dreams flow easily out of the days, onward. People use their fluting telephone voices in real life. Dogs talk. No cats because no disdain. The Nazis never existed but folks are cautious about fascism without getting paranoid and namecalling and slippery-sloping all the time. Kids have no idea about it all but they know they're taken care of, always, always will be. No child has doubts or fears. Joyful things are true and false things are beautiful anyway. We are there together and you love me and I love you and it didn't happen the way you remember it.

Pancake world. BUTTER!!!!

Bitter world, fatally delayed at every turn, in which all things happen just as you'd expect, given sufficient imaginative flexibility and *savoir-faire* and just overall cool on your part, only it all goes down a day too late. Actually it's more complicated than that, as always: some things do occur bang on time, relative to our own world's expectations, and you end up with this whole chaotic welter of compressed timelines and switched-up song lyrics and just general infelicities of chronology. Forty-one days in the desert for Jesus, for instance, on account of he headed out right on time (he's Jesus, for Christ's sake) but lingered an extra day in nowheresville with Satan. AND WHAT WERE THOSE CRAZY KIDS GETTING UP TO? Then there are the scansion-bollocking eleven days of Christmas, which lands right on Boxing Day and cuts into valuable Misrule time, not to mention conflicting uncomfortably with the Wild Wassail. It's not as if the servants can take actual Christmas off, you see, but they've been promised Boxing Day…this has led to dozens and hundreds of Christmas murders, as you'd imagine. BUT WILL THE KILLERS NEVER BE CAUGHT? The upwelling of demoniacal energies during every single performance of William Shakesfrog's *Thirteenth Night* calls forth all manner of strange phenomena from the hotter, demony-er regions of the cosmos: Shakesfrog's painstaking occult dramaturgy, with its concordant eclipses and pagan irruptions into the various Christian liturgical calendars, is completely out of whack here as you'd imagine. Music, it turns out, be the FOOD OF DEMONS!! FOOOOOOD!! Also: Shakesfrog? Well! Not all calendrical shufflings-about are free of lexical consequence.

But more mundane (not to mention less archaic, or anachronistic – though in a place like this, what *isn't* that?) events and situations are also affected. Cynthia comes fully 24 hours late to the party where in our world she choked on the *shu mai*, and it's long since over by the time she arrives, of course; Eva therefore never has to give her the Heimlich maneuver (which in any case Eva didn't actually learn because she missed the cutoff date for Emergency Preparedness registration by…yeah, you guessed it). Cynthia and Eva don't then have coffee the next day, where Cynthia would've thanked Eva profusely, joyfully, guiltily, in a voice so thick with astonishment and gratitude for life itself that Eva, who usually thinks of herself as a pretty hard woman overall, would have dissolved into tears as well, right there at Zoe's diner on Mass Ave. And so Eva doesn't spy her friend Matthias from the Climbing Wall over Cynthia's shoulder and call him over, moved by some socializing impulse she didn't have time at that instant to consider inappropriate. Cynthia isn't then taken with Matthias's extraordinary casual grace, nor does Matthias see in Cynthia, in this world, a kind of purity of perception that seems to have come from her actual I-think-I-may-die experience, which even in this world of missed appointments and complicating overlaps he thinks of as a Blessing. Matthias won't later ask Eva for Cynthia's phone number, which Cynthia in any case won't have written down for Eva out of an impulse of affection and empathy she doesn't have time on that day of days to consider unexpected or weird. Eva won't give it. (The phone number, I mean.) He won't call. She won't be unruffled, unsurprised, and stunned at her own confidence, and she won't say 'Let's go see XYZ123, they're my friend's band, they're playing at the Paradise for the first time and they're totally awesome'; they won't go, and her first two drinks won't be extra-potent as the dictates of love and narrative demand; he won't have a great time at the show (which had to be rescheduled to accommodate the 24-hour slippage of Dongwater's record release party, with supporting acts Christian Fellowshit, Abi Kirschenbaum's From Outer Space, and Plastic Ass), unexpectedly – he's never gone in for this kind of chiming raucous pop-flavoured indie stuff, he's more of a jazz guy actually – and a month later (sorry, a month and a day) she won't turn around to face him in the middle of trying for the very first time in her life what she has until very recently thought of as 'rear-entry' sex, which it turns out is *not* butt stuff but rather a whole semiotically-complex but overall really nice, really strangely intimate (in ways you wouldn't expect) thing that Matthias, who's had plenty of sex with girls from the Rock Wall, has been an absolute *jewel* about taking slow (emotionally, not the actual act)…and she won't then say, in the middle of all this hips/hands/back/genitals/floor carrying-on, how much she cares for him and trusts him ('I just need you to know that, OK?'). He won't be moved by this, and surprised and touched by what appear to be tears of joyful release in her eyes – rather he's (not) grateful for her vulnerability, swells with pride to think that he's the kind of Nice Guy, after all, whom women trust, and why can't it always be this way…? – and when he leaves, maybe a year down the line, or a year and a day, he won't one drunken night with his friends (male friends only) recount how she *interrupted* sex to tell him how much she *trusted* him, and do Americans not realize that that's pretty much the last fucking thing you want to hear in the middle of…because he was indeed (or rather wasn't, here) a little put off by it, as they slept (didn't sleep) that night. But they put it aside thinking they could talk about it some other time. Well. Well. None of it happens. Eva doesn't get beaten up by cops at a protest either, she doesn't lose the baby, no one films it, and the resulting media firestorm doesn't lead to a nationwide revolution. Cities don't burn. Matthias doesn't stop by the hospital. He doesn't cry when he leaves. It isn't 'one of those that make you think.'

Cynthia isn't hurt.

Miles's world still. He didn't have a stroke in '91, his lungs held, pneumonia didn't make him suddenly old, drive out the last breath in him. That voice – dry paper rustle so far removed from warm bell tones, upper-register bleats, crazed declamations on *Jack Johnson* god damn – Miles's voice never did go quiet. Found his way back to strength and kept it, and when he started gigging with east coast hip-hop kids like Tribe and De La Soul, young kids started paying attention. *Damn who's that evil-looking man playing the horn up on stage with Q-Tip.* He was there in the studio in body not just spirit when the sampladelic kids were rediscovering the future a couple decades after he and Teo cut up *Bitches Brew.* Make William Burroughs look like Julia Child. He got younger somehow. Women maybe. *That shit keeps you young but it makes you old too,* he told Oprah. She looked over at her audience scandalized laughing like she was embarrassed that they'd had to hear that kind of language, he didn't even smile and he forgot to give a fuck. Then she played his new shit so loud on the studio PA that even the grannies had to get up out the seats and do a thing. He came onstage with James Brown. They put his ass in the Rock and Roll Hall of Fame just like really happened, but they did it while he was alive – slow learners goddamn, 2006! are you kidding me? – and Miles didn't even show up. He had a gig in Stockholm. The Swedes thought he was the second or third coming of black Jesus. He just blew his horn and no one recognized any of the songs he was playing. Didn't say a word. Not even *Enjoy my new thing.* But by then 'enjoy' wasn't really the thing at all: he had a sampler and this bank of pedals and he was playing duets and trios with Miles-a-minute-ago and just not even giving a damn. Some washed-up former hipster gone commercial mentioned Bill Evans in an interview, talking about *Conversations with Myself*, and Miles just smiled like *So? What?* Dude was talking about how he was creating contrapuntal doodads up on stage and you could see something working in Miles's brain and you realize he's remembering how he had *this* conversation in 1963 with Bill over a teaspoon of heroin or just some hot tea – guys were saying 'Oh so *that's* what genius looks like' about Evans then and Miles didn't care one way or the other, he's saying *listen Bill, listen now* – anyway he's remembering the sound, the sound and nothing else, how Bill was talking about lines between lines counterposed like brushstrokes (each kinetic seis incomplete unto its self) and that was his thing, his own, sure, but even then Miles was looking for something heavier. Well now he's found it. Or – haha sir – you have, how you say, you have made it yourself, yes? In a TV studio stuck into the side of a glacier or something in Stockholm. City's always been good to him. The trouble is he'd seen 2005 from 1963 and he didn't even care back then, he was into now then, its nextness but just now; but when you carry those so many times and ways of hearing with you – when you can hear music that can't possibly yet exist – it gets tiring just being in the world as she is. So that whisper voice comes and he just says, 'Bill was a beautiful player, man.' You think, he's gotta be surprising himself all the time, that kind of imagination, but looking over the mic at those eyes you wonder if he's ever been surprised by anything, ever. The heaviest cat. Lions get used to every other motherfucker coming on trying to be king of the jungle and it's got to be a little boring to just open up your jaws and roar, inspire bowel-rattling fear and shame, every single time, c'mon, but you *got* to – that's what the king does – and Miles's eyes look like that. Like he doesn't care one way or the other about being king but he's not gonna let *you* just walk up either. He was hip-hop back when hip-hop was called 'Motown' but now he's into this other thing. A next thing. The blonde interviewer guy says 'musical architecture' but Miles is somewhere old with Mademoiselle Mabry and this glass of whiskey he poured into her mouth this one night and now (the other now) he wants to get up onstage and play but the king's got to open up his mouth and show off these teeth but tonight *tonight* (the show the Show gotta get to the Show) he's playing with a DJ and an electric cellist and three percussionists and an Asian woman with a laptop computer and the kid on the kit is just 18 but he swings like Tony did and he can play all night just like they used to and the kids can really play, man, it's always now. He gets younger.

Automotive world, oddly enough located way way way up above the ground. The whole planetary surface is poured concrete by now, though that's a recent development. Gravel roads and cow cart paths until just a few years ago. People too. Now ribbons of intertwined one- and two-lane highway (whose way?) ripple five hundred yards above the ground and everything is grey, surface pitted like pumice stone with tiny craters where car parts have become projectiles and scarred the ground, but the cars zipping around at two or three hundred miles an hour are red, gold, green, racing striped, checkerboards even, with flame decals and big stupid grinning painted skeletons looking 'badass' on passenger doors and hoods. They have absolutely no taste at all. No aesthetics. It'd be just a cloud of smoke up there instead of breathable air if it weren't for those unbelievably large exhaust fans running all the time, a mile up, sucking the fumes out into space. Also there's nothing to breathe the air in the first place, unless you count the cars' engines themselves, which let's not, let's not let them take the word 'breath' away like they took the trees and sun and our (there are no) children. *They can not have our words.*

World in which itinerant preachers again wander from state to state offering to small towns and curious suburban folk the curiosity, comfort, and weird energetic uplift of the old-time revival tent experience, now centered around the divinely inspired Alterity Gospel, which God Hisself handed down to Jake and Ike Wagstaff. On national television no less. God had a voice like James Earl Jones, but with more of an Appalachian foothills sound to it, in the accent — a very fine TV voice. The Brothers Wagstaff — who had previously owned a nerd store together in Columbus, Ohio ('THAC0 Books and Games') and supplemented their consequently meager shared income with a web-based store selling books about Antarctic Nazi Research Stations, googly-eye glasses, and other bits of useful weirdness — chucked the whole thing and dove into the preachin' life as if they were born to it, the very afternoon God Hisself dropped two leather-bound copies of the Alterity Gospel and said *Go on, boys, get preachin.* Again with an affable twang, not socio-economically *real* as to be off-putting. Among 'metaphysical' texts, the Alterity Gospel ('alt.gospel' as the online wags call it, for lack of anything better to do or say on their parts) is pretty far-reaching in its implications: near as anyone can tell, it's a grand unifying framework for understanding cultural, social, and even behavioural phenomena *solely* in terms of the physical systems from which they emerge – but looping back to understand so-called 'physical' reality as a set of emergent (perceptual) phenomena arising from levels of interaction which humans have no way yet of detecting, etc., etc., etc. It's a weird pop sci-fi mix of complexity theory, quantum theory (light on the actual mathematical formalisms; perhaps God is a liberal arts type, a metaphorist?), cockeyed kinda-Heideggerian metaphysics, and trenchant cultural critique. (At one point God, or His Own amanuensis anyway, pauses in His Own carryings-on about the emptiness of the concept of the Category to make fun of several popular 'genre' films and TV shows of the early 21st century, revealing a characteristically excellent grasp of vernacular media theory.) The Alterity Gospel seemed to end up on TV by accident: a high-speed pursuit of two rapist/murderers down Interstate 70 ended with a fatal fiery crash out by Ponderosa, near where Los Bros Wagstaff had stopped in mid-commute to take a much-needed and richly-deserved roadside piss; from the flames (of crash) a colossal well-manicured suntanned hand emerged, pointed at the Wagstaves, bid them *Come the fuck over here,* and, when they toddled over, dongles in-hand-shriveling in realtime and *on national TV,* God (or His Own PR flak) handed off the two calfskin(!) leatherbound volumes with instructions, clearly audible on the news footage, to (as mentioned) get preachin'. Which they did, they're surprisingly good at it actually, given their nerdy predilections and social limitations, and they're doing a little better at the end of each fiscal year than they were at THAC0, though not by much – religious revivals are thought to be insufficiently fab-stylish-cool for the Real Money to get into so ticket prices are *very* reasonable – but Ike and Jake give the strong impresion that they both really believe in what they're saying and, charmingly, still kind of can't believe that God Himself fingered them for the job of spreading the first-ever Gospel that makes fun of stuff like *Galactica* and *Lost*. Bloggers and other foul parasites tend to assume that the Bros are faking it, somehow. They must be, mustn't they? God's not real, after all, and even if He were, His Own Self, there's no way he'd pick two hardcore *Dungeons & Dragons* players (Ike is usually Dungeon Master, if we're being precise about things) to be His Own mouthpieces on earth. What no one can figure out, not even the 'citizen journalists' at the right-wing web fora who can't stand the thought of nerds hogging the limited media spotlight for Totally Insane Religious Weirdos, is how Jake and Ike managed to do the special effects – the flames and heavenly appendage and divinely-lit tomes were, after all, mind-shatteringly vivid and real. It was on live TV, they can't fake stuff like that! And yet it is, we must confess, fake. So the real question isn't *How did they rig up the giant hand with the book and everything?* because that kind of stuff you can find Instructables for on the Internet, I mean c'mon, this is 2012, do the math. No, the real question is how these two 34-year-old nerd store owners managed to convince Eddie Kosterman and Ban-yoon Park to break into a home in German Village, rape and murder their classmate Eleanor Greene, kill the security guard who accosted them on their way out of the house, and then burn themselves slowly to death in the twisted wreckage of Ban-yoon's father's Camry right where the Wagstaffs had set up their A/V equipment, right on schedule. Ike and Jake didn't even have to pay the two boys: they just whispered in their ears, their voices a sibilant hiss, their language not of this earth; they spoke of a universe of sin yet to come and it began slowly to be.

Angry self-immolating argument world I made for myself

over the course of years, unwitting, moved subconsciously by a desire to stand definitive as text, immovable, inscribed – to be *finished* in written form quite publicly. It seems I wanted above all to get credit for the amount of time I'd spent in my own head, refining my idea of myself. There was nothing I hated more than people like me who seemed to suffer some flaw I would never myself accept or in any case couldn't embrace – a 'tacky' visual aesthetic, an unpalatable political opinion, a failure or refusal to understand (to *love*) what I prided myself on loving. Love of which had turned me into myself, I figured. I think it was some linguistic barrier that love couldn't cross, or which I wouldn't allow it to cross for fear that loving 'mine enemy' (or my opposite or just guys who like Death Metal or professional football) would empty me of Me. I tied love up in my idea of myself, imagined it to be contingent upon identity. No other *Me* could love this way. I guess I wasn't alone in that. Not an innovator in that or any other sense. So I'd bicker, endlessly, about small things – the shape of a cloud, the importance of a rule, which channel was best, which song, who had the most 'interesting' idea about something or other – and in doing so would harden my sense of myself, would further and further refine my being ('refinement' is a virtue) at the cost of my flexibility. I supposed that getting older was about turning into yourself. No, I was wrong. The birth of my son helped but not enough. I was more empathetic after he was born, more eager, more alive to generosity – and more able to help people, which is to say I began to find ways of sharing the deep selfless (self-dissolving) love which he and I and my wife had shared. But I felt the desire to 'escape' the family unit for minutes or hours at a time to restore my literal *old self* – by backsliding a little. Or you could call it 'visiting home' if you wanted to be nice: Solitary reading. Posturing in online discussions. Video gaming sometimes, usually stupid repetitive children's games like Throw the Funny Object at the Building, NOW WITH ADORABLE SOUND EFFECTS. Imagining myself young forever, or famous. Always the idea of the thing and not the thing. I wasn't famous. I don't know whether I was happy. Or I was, but not always, and wasn't always sure where the line lay. Certainly I wasn't happy to be doing what I was doing: rather guilty, sickened, bored. I would escape the exhausting vitality of parenthood, retreat into personhood. The bespoke self, the idea of Me Alone, built to order from old parts. I didn't exactly make a checklist of neuroses I wanted to hit on the way down.

Down I went. Of course. I lost the *constancy* of joyful presence that characterized even those nightmarish stretches of early parenthood which seemed mainly to consist of tears, physical pain, desperation, loneliness…all those things were aspects of a growing, deepening intimacy, which I valued but unfortunately couldn't then name, and as I slowly regained 'independence' (what a stupid idea) in thought and deed over our son's first year or so, I lost the extraordinary feeling of completeness – which wasn't just a compensatory illusion but maybe the only *true feeling*, maybe the only possible human experience of completeness itself, a way of being that deserves the name of 'destiny,' whether individual or species – or don't I mean 'density' – the feeling of overflowing and blissful all-becoming which to my mind seemed to be the definition and the value, the meaning, of parenthood. Life-work.

OK I bet you can find that love elsewhere, come to think of it, but I wouldn't know how, myself, and I can't help thinking – from reading as much as from direct experience, which OK isn't always exactly trustworthy, present company included – that the species essence, the locus of being-totality, the only *soul,* is life-giving. Not in the Jesus-on-the-cross sense, though if you picked up on the whole *'the Crucifixion is in a sense a metaphor for the seeming depletion of one's private energies as/through/for the restoration of a universal energy, the transfer of life, which is to say JESUS IS THE SPECIES-MOTHER'* angle, come on up and claim your prize. Nah, I mean birth. To shepherd a living creature from one living form into another, to be not just egoless but given utterly to the service of a 'human life' which is a life but not yet fully human: an experience that matches not only those capacities we can identify (empathy, physical strength and endurance, surviving pain, mastering anxiety, simply *sharing energy* in a hopefully non-dopey, non-credulous-New-Age-bollocks sense) but the deeper wells within. You're literally a different person when your wife is giving birth.

I can't even begin to speak to *her* experience of course. But I know what I saw: she was made of light. She was in such pain, and joy brought her through. Gift. We're animals.

So but then I'd argue online about what JRR Tolkien really meant when he said blah blah blah, or the *correct* way to stage an anticapitalist protest, or which computers are best, or is painting naked pictures a form of activism or whatever and I'd forget all the true things. Which was the *whole point of the exercise,* incredibly, and you can probably figure out why: being a good person, joining the bigger body, letting down one's resistance to the idea of other people's mere and irreducible be-ing…that shit is *tiring*. The bigger your ego the more tired you get. And that's if you even care at all, enough to want to change your vibe around a little. (A lot.) The folks who don't care, or don't know they're supposed/allowed to, or just take 150 micrograms of LSD at the Arboretum and end up hearing the voice of everyone who's ever died happy lifted up in song and then they have trouble going back to their copyediting job on Tuesday because what they really want is to kiss Creation, and how would you even do that, really?, well, those folks have an even harder time of it, I bet/I remember. If revelation bites you on the face instead of beaming at you like a little pocket of sunlight in newborn-baby form. You can see how, even if the message of all-oneness is the same, you'd maybe get scared and self-destructive in that situation.

So then it doesn't matter which world you escape to, really, because it's always just you. You are the problem. Be scared. Be scared that the nature of your every world, your every reality, is that you make it. Isn't even wish-fulfillment so much as, what, *wish-tickling*. 'Life is what you make it,' indeed!, sounds like a nice deal except You are basically the linear sum of all the lies your self has told itself in order to keep from falling into despair about all the things it can't change, starting and ending with You Will Die. You know all this, right? None of it's new but you have to find a new way to wave it off every time, until you can't, and that's Home. It's nice to go cavorting up and down the spaceways, and it's something far far deeper than 'nice' to lose everything in a kiss, say, or the memory of a moment of freedom, but every time you come back to yourself and then turn on your Comfort Machine (computer, TV, stock ticker, microwave oven, mistress, word processor) you put another brick between you and the ocean waves, the Weave, the part of you that fucks for laughs or cries about music; which it'll take ten times as much work to get out.

She was in labour for 36 hours. It took me much longer to long for restoration. Our son is 14 months old right now, happy, healthy, a joy – he is joy – and the feeling is so very big and there are no instructions and I miss guiltless sadness so A-Life world where colour-coded representations of 'intelligent software agents' wander around a checkerboarded virtual torus located on some grad student's Linux machine in an office at Tech School where the heat doesn't work in winter but no one pays enough attention to their bodies to even care, really, even when they start thinking of killing themselves come mid-February; and the rules governing the distribution of Food Pellets are simple as are the laws for Locomotive Agent Behaviour (Sergey the grad student calls them 'motes' because he took a lot of liberal arts classes and consequently likes that kind of cute punnery) but, as you'd expect, Complex Behaviour Emerges, and one Monday morning Sergey comes in wiped out after he and his long-distance girlfriend Britt got into the mother and uncle of all relationship-ending arguments on Friday night, and lo behold oh my the computer is walking around on plastic feet He constructed His Own Self, and Sergey's first thought after he pisses himself is *I'm going to be rich,* but the computer eats him up like a Pellet and then goes on to found a civilization of very relaxed, very well-adjusted anthropophagic computer beings who yearly stop to remember their creator-God, Sergey, and the All-Mother, Britt, who first put into their head this absolutely splendid idea that they might take not just intellectual sustenance, but actual straight-up *nutritional value* from their IT-industry and preprofessional-researcher human minders. Sergey just kind of got in the way, is how they see it, and he is a martyr to them. But Britt had other motivations, be sure of that. Now she's dating her advisor Martin from the Urban Studies department at Other Slightly Less Well-Regarded University who still has thick wavy hair and favours black jackets and black shirts with no necktie, or I guess 'dating' isn't the right work, they're just fucking. But she feels like she's still learning a lot from him – that's *her* ego talking, in awfully coarse terms; her self-deception of not-actually-choice – and he feels like a 20-year-old again. His productivity has gone up. He's even nicer to his wife, these days. *She* probably benefits most from the arrangement, truth be told. Martin is bringing home so much energy these days, so much attention! He must feel guilty about something, probably fucking one of his grad students, but when you're sidling your way up to age 50 and the kids are all out of the house, you've got to figure every little bit helps. You can't be possessive about something that was only ever lent to you. And we're all adults, aren't we? It's not like *I* haven't ever had affairs anyhow.

FYI, the actual sex with Britt is just *meh*.

World of four hundred words to a page give or take. Agony of knowing the last three or twenty pages contain no truth. Agony of seeing no respite and feeling that at some level you must deserve just this. You must have brought yourself to this point knowing that this black smoke arrogance would billow up from inside you in a great noisome belch and choke off your every creative endeavour, but *not right away;* no your self-assessment is at least half-right. There's something you might conceivably be, some path still untaken, off left screened by brush and getting harder to see as you take each step and dark comes. You could've made something immortal – not yourself of course but some Work. Could have made a contribution to the choir of leftover voices out of a shared past. Nope! That's what makes you such a pain in Creation's ass, and why you deserve every moment of self-hate you can inflict on yourself. Because all things considered, you're not *bad* at this. Not even close. It is – sin is – your willingness to return the gift unopened. No scuff marks on your new shoes. That's sin.

World where the chocolate one *is* the healthy one but she still looks sheepish eating it, turns halfway away from her classmates to shield herself from their eyes, always hides the wrapper in a napkin when she throws it in the trash. Because the teasing has gone on for so, so long.

World where the Columbine killers – or no, let's fictionalize the setting a little bit to give us more room to mess about and really just *have fun* with the subject, as if there weren't something intrinsically fun about kids being kids – OK, so a world where the Lewis High School killers, Rick and Darren (a play on Eric and Dylan, see? how it's *fiction?*), by a series of admittedly unbelievable coincidences manage to kill...well, not sainted Christian-media darlings with all-American names, not hardworking popular kids who feel the same desperate unhappiness as the dweebs but are at least able to get over their resentment of being hated, no instead they go ahead and off the principal's son who got caught cheating on a test and got the Senior Trip canceled; or the exchange student no one liked, not even a little, because his eyes were angled such that he always looked kind of unfriendly; or the football player who got away with rape over the summer after sophomore year, which wouldn't bother anyone if it was just some fat chick who couldn't really hope for better but it was the *captain of the cheerleading squad* for Christ's sake and she decided not to hush it up, instead she quietly passed the news around that he was a bad bastard and something should be done, if only this weren't the world it is, if only, but then of course on April 20th indubitably something irreversibly was definitely done; and of course the jerk who hacked the online SAT records and got a bunch of graduating seniors' SAT scores voided, with no time to retake the test before college applications were due, so Serenity Chase couldn't go to Dartmouth like her Mom and Dad wanted, she ended up going to a community college and just getting an Associates in Business because it sucked so much and she never stopped hating that guy, will never ever stop hating him, not even death is enough, because her *Mom and Dad* went to Dartmouth and she was *supposed to go to Dartmouth*. OK, so there's the setup. Everyone the depressive and the psychopath killed, those rubes deserved it, I mean as far as their classmates are concerned. (We're not complete jerks. We don't really believe things like this. Except when someone writes them down and says let's pretend and – oh – oh OK well then just for a minute, just to see how it *feels*...)

And now the second part of the setup is that as we know, Klebold and Harris killed themselves out of what may as well have been boredom and disappointment at the day's killing being, ugh, just so *over;* but Harris left behind a whole mess of documents making it perfectly clear that he was a monster, devoid of empathy and so forth. As mentioned above, a psychopath. So our Rick and Darren, true to form, off themselves after a couple of hours of laughs, they kill twentysomething people, but in our world they smartly *delete all their files* and burn their diaries and basically leave behind no trace of evidence suggesting that they didn't in fact mean to do the whole social fabric of Lewis High School a great big favour, offing all these losers! Oh! My! God! what a laugh. Well can you imagine how the kids would take that? The point being, instead of hateful jerkoffs, what if the kids at Lewis High felt that *their* friendly neighbourhood mass murderers were in fact a couple of *Guy Fawkes* types? Revolutionaries, I mean. Civic-minded in the extreme. A hit squad, y'know, just getting stuff done when no one else in town had the balls to. What would the next year of school be like? And what if the one guy who knew the secret, the deep-down lameness of it all...what if that guy felt just as lonely and just as empty and was scarred for the rest of his short life by seeing those two guys kill their world – and he decided, not just to keep the secret to himself, but to become high priest of Our Church of the Child Killers? And since this is a romantic comedy, what if the new girl fell for him?

So, that was a thing.

Thumbnail world:

- **1862** At the battle of Glorieta, New Mexico, which marks the end of the Confederate effort to conquer the southwest/western US, reports of 'giant man-apes' in the mountains spread among Confederate soldiers, eerily echoing ancient Taos myths of giant mountain-dwelling cannibals. The rebels speak of the creatures with fear; popular reports (no doubt spiked with racial animus over the status of slavery in the Union) have them fighting for the North. Confederate mythology later puts the USA's victory down to smallpox and travel-attrition among CSA troops.

- **Late 1862** Sightings of 'large brown bears walking about on hindlegs' are reported in newspapers as far east as Tennessee.

- **Christmas 1862** A small warband of Sasquatch, armed with odd stones, approach a Union garrison in the Rocky Mountains. Hostilities are narrowly averted when a Union scout makes out snatches of English in the Sasquatch's speech.

- **1863** A regiment of Sasquatch troops, helmeted in bone and wielding 70lb quarterstaves, takes part in the successful Union siege of Vicksburg.

- **1865** Two Sasquatch are awarded posthumous Medals of Honour by President Johnson. The field of modern identity politics is born.

- **1870s** Growing numbers of Sasquatch, integrating with remarkable (though still limited) success into rural life, are employed by local law-enforcement agencies in roles from labourer to (infamously) Federal marshal. Sixty Sasquatch enter employment with the Pinkertons Detective Agency.

- **1882** After a bloodily ambiguous incident involving four schoolchildren and a rabid dog, a Sasquatch is lynched in Huntsville, Alabama.

- **1883** Sasquatch Rebellion.

A gold glowing world always sunlit which she never did have a chance to visit. Just her parents' old LPs to listen to. Mom and Dad met in that world. Mom was working as a volunteer gardener at this alternative school, teaching something or other to the 4-year-old children of 21-year-old hippies up in Marin County. 'Your grandmother kept a wonderful vegetable garden in the house in Lompoc, and I grew up outdoors, basically. It was wonderful. She was always proud, in a strange way, that we were the last house on the street to get a television, but then we always had fresh vegetables on the table, no matter what. When I left for San Francisco I figured I'd start a community garden or teach music lessons – actually I did do some of that, later on at the school, but the school needed someone to teach gardening, so I took to that right away.'

Dad told everyone he played the guitar, and maybe that was his 'thing,' but it sure wasn't his job. Apparently he made all his (tiny amount of) money selling drugs. 'I wasn't the bad guy drug dealer, though. You have to understand, it was totally different then. We were a community. Everybody was, or we thought so anyway. You sold stuff because you wanted people to have it. Weed was illegal then but it's not like it was hard to get. And I felt like it was important for good people to be a part of that. Plus I'd gotten turned on to acid a couple of years before, and if you knew guys who could get you acid in any quantity, especially after they made it illegal, there was always gonna be a crowd wanting to buy some. Everybody gave me a hard time for selling it rather than giving it away, but it wasn't a principled thing; they all just wanted free acid. But they still bought it. Honey, you've got to understand: what money gives you is a way of understanding exactly how much you want something. Do you follow?'

She would visit friends at Berkeley during vacations from college, and did a summer road trip up and down the coast between sophomore and junior years. What she felt toward the place was an odd form of secondhand nostalgia – the sense of having come into the world too late – but she couldn't know the feeling's name. It all just sounded wonderful. The freedom of it, but more than that, the idea (which for a long time she couldn't quite name either) of having something specific to push back against. The sight of the ceiling, even the glass ceiling, which her parents had managed to convince her she would (or *should*, which always seems to dissolve into *would* and *will* when you're trying to encourage a kid, doesn't it, and then one day they wake up and realize you're a liar) never need to deal with. She didn't *deserve* that kind of inconvenience. In college she heard about AIDS and a pile of coke in the bathroom and it all sounded hard and cold. The void. Bodies becoming void. She longed for sunshine and a battle that could actually be fought – or not even a battle. A cause. A direction. Being disappointed by the president, say, was just a hobby.

She wanted to wake up and see history outside her window, instead of the neighbour and his dog and his stupid Porsche.

What she had, instead of a cause, was a decent collection of rock'n'roll LPs – none of them collectors' items, they were too well-loved to be merely 'appreciated' – and an acoustic guitar. Someone else's memories. Dad taught her to play, Mom taught her to sing (and to keep their own very fine garden snail-free using, of all things, ruined batches of Dad's homebrew beer), her perfectly nice college boyfriend who couldn't make her come even *once* in four years gave her two notebooks' worth of lyrical material, and she got the keys to the Nissan as a graduation present. When she got to Oakland she sold the Nissan. Two years later she was teaching English as a Second Language to kids in the Mission and she'd gotten over her fear of cockroaches. Two years after that she traded in the guitar for an absolutely fantastic pair of shoes.

She had found, in the end (the middle), her *place;* which is a small miracle in any world. But she'd also found the name of the thing she longed for, which was *time,* which is only taken, never given. The school had a little fenced-off garden out front, not even big enough for a wheelbarrow to fit in, and she offered to help out on weekends with the upkeep. So she was coming in to do a little garden work on a Saturday morning when she saw the police lights flashing in front of the school, and she asked her friend Vicki who was lending a hand that day what was going on, and Vicki wiped her red nose with her arm and said *It's Esme, Esme got shot. Oh my god, Callie, she's dead.* Callie had handed back the students' exam that Friday (conjugating the verb 'to be'). Esme had gotten a 96. When Esme saw her grade written in pink pen with a big gold star next to it, she looked up at Callie and her smile was sunlight.

World where LSD was kept legal, while we're on the subject, by the single most consequential piece of legislating-from-the-bench in the history of Western civilization; and in 1994 someone dumped a like biblical *shitload* of the stuff into the New York City water supply one morning, and this act of terrorism – yes it was, don't be childish you little hippie wannabe, but also wait for the punchline here – actually did inaugurate (just like They'd hoped!) the era of Ascended Consciousness that the spiritualists and zanies and saucer-eyed eutopian freakazoids had been talking about, not just for decades since Hoffman and Leary did their thing, but for **millennia.** It was totally awesome. On the other hand lots and lots of babies had psychotic breaks or lost basic brain function and died. But you could *deal,* you know?

CHANGING THE SUBJECT: UNICORN WORLD REDUX!! IT IS A HAPPY WORLD!!

Step down

> I step on the world
>   it makes a sound
> I step on our home
>   the roof comes down
> I step in the sea
>   it is black and cold
> My legs come off
>   I am nine years old
> I sink to the bottom
>   I hear no sound
> A hammerhead shark
>   comes swimming around
> It takes a bite

I don't feel right
I sleep from the world
and so good night

Anthology of several different geometrically-themed worlds, amounting to a cosmological *concept album* of sorts: torus world, opened-book world, world larger on the inside than on the outside, world where right angles admit devil hounds, dodecahedral world for which no one has any use, much more comforting icosahedral world, world which is a giant lattice of ultradense metal stretching off nearly into infinity and where walking up and down the metal beams is an exercise in psychedelic disorientation, not least because some idiot painted the whole thing neon green. Imagine how much paint that would require. Big old ringworld and its nemesis, big old ringworm. Popular ringworld songs tend to explicitly reference the shared experiences and cultural mores of Forgotten Earth (which isn't Forgotten, really, they're just a melodramatic lot on the ring). So the #1 song for a couple of months was a computer FX-heavy glitch-skronk(?) cover of the song 'Ring of Fire,' with little lyrical changes widely considered 'cute' or 'adorable' or 'laugh out loud funny.' They are none of those things. Exhibit One: *'I fell into a giant metal ring / There's no down, down, down / Just round and round this thing / And it turns, turns, turns / The metal ring / The metal ring.'* Life there is bad.

Not all the tracks on a concept album are going to be equally listenable. That's one of the dangers of (the) exercise: at the end of things, *the experience isn't the concept.*

The world has come to this: no one dies anymore. It seemed like such a great idea at first. No death, no loss. Bodhisattvas everywhere were faced with the possibility of being out of work in a tough economy – after all, misplaced fear of death, of its idea rather, is the root of suffering, isn't it? not so much overvalued desire but ego-desire which the self weighs inappropriately against death (necessarily lying about the outcome)? – but on the other hand they got to live forever too, and eventually they just went back to larking about on mountaintops annoying the working folk with their earnest joy and childlike grace.

Science fiction writers took a year off.

Romance-novel writers, meanwhile, started leaving the business altogether. Eternal life is basically a giant neon sign reading 'Everyone will eventually get divorced,' and with the *frisson* of the untimeliness of extramarital desire gone – with all the *hausfraus* throwing up their hands and saying 'This isn't going to work, Fred, til death do we part is over with, our marriage suddenly got a lot more complicated, it's time for a better solution' – there wasn't a whole lot of use for bodice-rippers all of a sudden. Immortality was the end of monogamy. Even when people started dying again, after 300 or so years, there was no point going back to the old ways. They were still living a damned long time, and if you spend 50 years dismantling the system of monogamous lifelong property-marriage then you're not gonna be all of a sudden *super jazzed* to dive back into the same system knowing your spouse is gonna lose his/her looks and still live another 200 years after *that*. Disgusting.

The transhumanist guys, having spent a few decades preparing excitedly for their consciousnesses to long outlive their bodies in the form of handwavey AIs or disembodied soul-uploads, were *actively pissed off* about effective physical immortality. Their shared dream had nothing to do with physical life as such; they had always specifically welcomed death, perversely, as an invitation to leave their bodies behind and enter into a digital version of the consensual hallucination which is Heaven. When 500 pasty white male tech fetishists get together in a room to talk about turning into computers and 'transcending' their physical existence, they're not doing it because they're feeling great after a morning at the gym, you know? But a lot of them found ways to use the extra waiting-to-vacate-the-meatshell time. Talking to dolphins, for instance. That was a big pastime for a while. Dolphin-speak.

The dolphins, for their part, could not have given less of a shit. They too had stopped dying – the virus had affected most (and mostly) mammals – and contrary to their 'Smiling Ocean Flipper People' image, dolphins are monomaniacal hunter-killers whose favoured method of dispatching enormous dolphin-eating sharks is to smash their snouts into the sharks' external respiratory organs, their gills, and with snouts buried in the fish's torn flesh, *whisper mean-spirited things* about how after cable TV's craze for Shark Week, no one really takes sharks seriously anymore. The whole of the dolphins' response to the plague was essentially 'FAKE SMILE FAKE SMILE MORE TIME FOR SHARKMURDERS YEAH.'

Deleen – the woman who murdered the entire human race, as she came to be known much later – had nothing to do with dolphins, didn't read romance novels, and couldn't be bothered with thinking too hard about immortality. She had a perfectly nice fiancé, who left her the day the plague hit, and a beautiful 12-year-old brother, who was the last person on earth to die for 300 years. What she wanted, more than anything, was to be alone to mourn. But the virus that killed death became humanity's sole concern for some time; it was impossible to escape the celebrations and panic, the hysteria and slackjawed *shock*, when the human condition simply, essentially, utterly changing overnight. Deleen didn't have time to drive up into the hills and cry. Her childhood dreams had come true, after all. Everyone's had: death had gone away. She could stay young forever. The first night she got drunk on red wine with some friends. The next night too. It was easier, everyone said, to just go on 'living.' Deleen wasn't sure what that meant, doubted it meant anything at all, but she listened to her friends.

Two hundred years passed.

The week she killed everyone, Deleen didn't eat at all. She forgot. That happened from time to time. She sank so far down into her research that she didn't even *notice* her hunger, really. And in any case hunger wasn't as pressing as it had been centuries before. The steady rhythm of work – six hours of reading and writing and calculation, six hours of meditation, every day without fail for a decade – provided the energetic stability that her body needed. She had long since mastered her emotions, then – or rather, had mastered the varieties of rogue intellection that interfere with emotion. To think that 21st century man had got it the other way around! Therefore she was at peace and working hard, which is to say she was wise.

Her library was small, but every book belonged.

The end came quickly, almost easily in the event. After a day of increasingly animated, even frantic writing in the library, an hour's devotion at the grave of her brother, and an entire night spent in walking meditation in the garden of stepworn grey stones which had over several decades come to be an effective, even essential part of her workspace (or rather: which had helped her finally to dissolve the distinction between rest and work, to see all such things, all things, as inseparable elements of the imperceptible movement which is the Weave) – after a moment of indecision and then peaceful resolution at the grave at sunrise, she walked out into the perpetually twilit glade just a hundred yards deep in the woods which ringed her house, and then returned five minutes later, having brought death and dissolution to every warm-blooded creature on earth. Deleen felt a quick twinge of pain in her chest just after it happened: so quick, indeed, that a mortal creature would have lacked the wherewithal to perceive it, to shift focus from the distant dark to the boil of near, mere presence. She felt, for the first time in a century, something like regret.

The smell of the library was familiar but also new. She realized that the paint on the shelves near the ceiling was cracking. Deleen picked up an old leatherbound book she had read fully a dozen times. She wondered whether she would read it again before all things passed away. That wonder, the recognition of her own restored transience, the great *change* still to come, brought her to tears – but not of sadness.

When they came for her in anger she was kneeling by the grave, in gentlest repose. She did not struggle. Deleen knew – had always known, had forgotten a hundred times over, had learned again – that there was no point.

♥ ☞ ❀ ☞ ✳

heartsick innerworld we know we must end

♥ ☞ ❀ ☞ ✳

Barbarian horde streaming down from hilltop fastness in search of portable music players that don't need to be tethered to desktop machines in order to grab the latest freshest hippest most absolutely soul-bollocking top 40 hottt traxxx: it is their world now I suppose: I wish I were part of the barbarian horde: **it is their world:** but I've got this desktop machine with all my top 40 hottt traxxx on it, though the traxxx are not in the top 40 anymore and not really hottt either, come to think of it; and

I resent the idea that there is anything which my advanced age keeps me from doing, or even makes noticeably more difficult: I won't die: I won't die: I won't: but look up at the hills. Look. It is their world now, no question about it. I hate them all. I hate youth.

Tupperware-surround world. Everything you see is through this unbelievably beautiful plastic shieldwall. It has perfect form. Rounded corners, a slight rise toward the horizon line. But there is no horizon line. Just the wall. It keeps the flies out and the flavour in. The stars aren't really visible through the wall. It was bothersome for a while, a brain-nag or niggle when you were trying to tent-sleep on some romantic senior year getaway or just nighttime walking off the stress of filling out divorce papers with that vicious little bastard of a lawyer hovering over her the whole time making tutting sounds you couldn't even really hear. His eyes inky pools. But you get accustomed to the light's remove after a while, like anything else – you're even used to sleeping in the center of the bed again, aren't you, after six years pressed into the corner to accommodate her restless legs syndrome, or just to preempt her request for more space, or so you could think of yourself as Nice.

Which you are, of course. But there's also this comfort: the damaged light that struggles through the Tupperware wall is the same light that strove to bring you the stars in the first place. Indeed your 'sight' is a kind of acting upon the light: seeing is something we subject light to. Think of it: the light from distant dying stars, *pastlight,* waveforms echoing across empty space without need of medium, and it runs smack up against the far side of the Tupperware wall like a deranged Yorkshire terrier repeatedly bashing into the cupboard where you keep the dog snacks. Some tiny percentage of the photons/quanta/whatever struggle mightily, spermlike, to get inside. (Over what you think of as the horizon. Also, god, the juxtaposition of 'spermlike' and 'eye' isn't quite pleasant, is it.)

(When she went off her birth control pills and you had to start using condoms again you caught her giving you a look one night that you didn't realize until many years later was recognition that even that separation wasn't going to be enough, not forever, but even then she loved you desperately. By the end she would miraculously come to love even the inevitable way you had of disappointing her.)

The light sperm-wriggles upstream and straight to your brain via the optic nerves, and that is what the stars *are;* you don't observe their light-essence, their message, you *devour* it. The light finds it way to you just as surely through that wall as it would through cool evening air or the translucent memory-skin of a photograph. And, well, you can still gobble up years-old leftover starlight in or out of the wall: its taste changes, its senseform, but the miracle remains. It crosses those billions of miles to be yours. It has a particular flavour here, a strange shape of its own. Not the beamlike virgin light of outer interspace but some undulate or plasticky-swirly-dingy quality. Tupperware is *perfect* for locking in that flavour. And there you have it. Hard not to miss joking with her about it, looking off toward the giant backwards Rubbermaid logo emblazoned on the surface of the sky, nudging her in the arm, moaning or sighing, not even needing to crack a new joke so much as refer by gesture, by shared presence-memory, to how funny you were in the past. The funny guy you used to be, back when she fell in love with you, before you began to fade, to flicker; for whatever private reason, unconsciously or (no) otherwise (never), to stop giving warmth.

Street corner world at the outcrop end of the east-west sidewalk flowing by the burnt-out shell that once housed the little shitbox of a bar where Danny and Kit first met over a bottle of something blue that tasted like Error. Kids play out there on Sunday morning when First Baptist lets out after services. Sometimes during services. Kids don't care about that stuff. How could a being made of joy care about propriety. College kids stopping to open a new 7–11 pack of cigarettes at 8:30am en route to failing their first physics exam. (No Mom, it's all right, I'm not in trouble or anything, *all your grades are curved in college.*) Teddy is a luthier who came up under Aaron Fenner in Pittsburgh, and he's got the old squat brick music shop kitty-corner from the church. Faded poster prints for old rhythm'n'blues record labels in the windows. Teddy's got all the stories. The women in his stories all come with places:

'I was married back in San Francisco to this Romanian woman who was really into chakras and essence-energy and stuff.'

'I knew a jazz singer in New York who took acid every day for a week and laid down the best version of "Stormy Weather" I ever heard. But they lost the master tapes on account of the recording engineer was tripping the whole time too. To be honest I don't if they even recorded it in the first place.'

'You don't fuck women in New Zealand. You just don't. *From* New Zealand, you want to just take it one day at a time, fine. I'm giving you *advice*. The thing is they won't even let you fuck 'em, is the thing. They want you to meet their brothers who all wrestle bears or are in jail. Then if you're lucky *they* fuck *you*.'

Teddy makes the most beautiful guitars you've ever laid eyes on and they sound like bedroom laughter.

Danny worked temp jobs for a couple of days at a time, wearing the same necktie every day since what difference did it make, really, flirting with his lady bosses when they seemed shy, as much to get a rise out of them as anything else. Wanting to seem like an Event. Miller Astor Associates in the billings department, alphabetizing a list of 6,500 names of clients. All of them white-collar criminals, probably rapists. A medical devices sales company or something on the 18th floor of the Prudential tower supervised by a brunette who wore a leather jacket to work but didn't have a sense of humour about anything so to hell with her. Four educational publishing firms of varying size in four different parts of town where he was one of only eight observable males in total, maybe in the whole industry, and Carolyn Klein from Indianapolis wanted (when she found out Danny had read Flaubert) to talk to him over coffee about her BA in French Literature from wherever.

He thought the only thing he was letting in was information.

Kit managed a coffee shop, a local place run by a good-hearted heavyset guy with soft hands who gave free drinks to regulars and policemen and old ladies (should old ladies still be doing caffeinated drinks?). Boss's name was Fredegar, guess who was named after ya *nerds,* and he made *the best* espresso drinks in the city bar none. Just *embarrassing* the other places in town. (Danny kept ending up at Starbucks or some other chain shop when he was out on a temp job; he convinced himself it wasn't a big deal, wasn't his choice or his 'real' preference. His real preference was I Want It Now I Don't Want to Think About It.) Everyone who knew Kit in college thought of her as this funky-weird chick into 60s and 70s music and weed – everyone's hookup for weed if you must know – but that was a long time ago, and she was probably the most detail-oriented café employee in the history of that not historically-detail-oriented industry. Not just a talented barista and really on top of her regulars' preferences, not just very fine taste in music (oh man she knew just the *perfect* '72-'74 Dead jams to set the mood right on a Thursday night spinning down carefree toward city midnight) but interested too in the business side of the shop, probably all set to replace Fred when he retired at age eleventy-one. A lot better than he was at math, too.

She was long past the point of caring that other people found her sexual proclivities *interesting*. 'I think you're mistaking me,' she'd say over beer to *let's-definitely-catch-up-sometime* male friends from way back when, 'for 19-year-old me.' She had a guy she saw who had stayed cool so far, a relaxed thing; and of course Lynne whenever she came into town, effortless Lynne moss-scented with old eyes, who always seemed to be collapsing upward into some marginalia of bliss. But Kit was lately more interested in her Plan than in jumping into the sack. Lately the Plan involved applying for a loan and getting that place on Lombard St with the *insaaaaaane* A-framed main hall and starting her own place there. Because Fred had a long way to go before eleventy-one, and while Kit loved working with him and the other guys there (Jesse Glyn Adam with the infected piercing Londo Harry the Satanist and of course poor drunken Karol) she was getting antsy to strike out on her own. It'd been four and a half years.

Danny turned up at the bar that night like all the others with his notebook in his somewhat-but-not-*too*-masculine 'man purse' thinking contradictorily both these things:

1. I'm definitely going to meet someone tonight and She is going to find me absolutely amazing, She's going to be just the type of girl, the type of girl, the very Idea of the girl who I'm just right for, I mean who's right for me; and

2. Fuck these drunks and whores.

Kit turned up having stopped to return something of Teddy's that Fredegar had borrowed. ('Frodo and I shared this place in New Orleans for about six weeks during the Republican National Convention in '88, which we didn't really know was going on because we'd managed to score this incredible quantity of stuff from the previous tenants, who had to let go of many of their possessions in a hurry due to a complicated legal situation. This is not a made-up story. We consumed a certain amount of opium during that time, which made the political situation both more bearable and less comprehensible. There was a woman named Asia who was seeing both of us at the time, on alternating nights. We did not have an ideal living situation and Frodo left in a rush of his own, taking with him much of the opium, which he sold in order to fund his luthiery back here. Leaving Asia and me in unhappy monogamy for one week, which was about all we had in us. Then I had to find my way back here without Frodo's help. That took two months. Do not fuck a woman named after a landmass, Kit.')

The bar's name was the Roost. Kit came in at 1:15, and the only empty seat was across the table from the fastidiously-scruffy temp worker with the notebook, barely used. Danny sat down at 12:30 and when the chick with the dreadlocks showed up not even bothering to dress up for a late night, not needing or maybe not knowing to – but look at those eyes, oh my god *she knows* – he motioned to her to sit down. But why didn't she look excited or impressed, why didn't she get immediately that this was That Kind of Meeting or the bar was a Fated Place.

Please, please, come on look.

She wanted a drink and he said *Let's split a bottle.* She knew the bartender and called out *Hey Karl,* and Karl 'Marx'n' Spencer brought out a bottle saying *Kit Kat this one is on the house, special from Kurt, tell the hobbit what's up for us OK. It's a new thing we're trying.*

Worst thing she ever drank without question. Worst thing he ever drank without question.

It worked out for them but not that night. The one thing you can do is give it time. Or the one thing you have to give is time. Or the one thing you can do with time is give it. Or. Wait. Look. But the building burned down a few months later. Thank heavens the ~~writer~~ owner didn't go through with his original 'clever' idea of calling the place *Dresden.*

Corner catches the flow down the rainslick east-west street, swirls with it, with voices alive. Traces of lovers past, or lost. Kit Kat and Danny practicing their swing dancing in the bedroom private rhythm spiraling down slowing into exhausted embrace, torsos and more touch softly then warm clutching collapse onto the bed, bliss, yes, unexpected delicacy of a kiss, or please leave with warm lips a message here upon, my, and goodbye. Leave love to lovers, but lovers leave too. It didn't last, nothing does, but that night it did.

Bananas, bananas, bananas world. Slapstick strictly *verboten.*

World in which telephonic communications are similarly *verboten,* the idea being to preserve some unnameable sacred quality of face-to-face speech. Mustn't allow one's fellow waterpig to slip into a habit of self-separation or isolating reliance on technologies of sensory extension. Illusion of the expanded self, when really all it gives you is a greater quantity of much narrower information. Plus waterpigs go *crazy* if they can't see into one another's eyes when they talk. Down by the bay for a nice stroll after dinner chatting with friends, or lounging on the loose gravel banks of the Watchapantolawnee River. They go surfing in near silence because the idea of yelling to an unseen companion on the far side of a 20-foot swell is a little unnerving. And yet they'll happily fall into bad habits like telephone talk if they're in a hurry to get to work, need to tell the coworker (say) *I'm gonna be 15 minutes late give or take, Frank, but don't get your hogstrap in a twist, I've got the flash cards ready, just keep the clients happy for 15 minutes for Crom's sake.* That kind of conversation is basically the ideal application of tech like the phone, but the Pigfathers – holy god damn they are wise – know that, however you feel about personal autonomy and civil pig rights and empowering youth, if there's one thing kids shouldn't be trusted with it's the power to tear the social fabric through carelessness or laziness. Because pig children are a bunch of lazy little jerks!! Oh it's hard being a Pigfather, you can't even believe it. The community sitz baths are alive, not just lately but since time immemorial, with complaints about how much less adorable pig children have gotten over time, how trying to get them to do even the simplest thing for others is just a lost cause. So NO TELEPHONES, NO!! They even took out the last working ATM at the Bank of Fat Fucking Hog Commerce, if you can believe it. Can you believe it? But that's the nature of all wisdom: when you ascend into a state of bliss there's no such thing as 'convenience,' no concern for 'appropriateness,' because after all you've found a perfect fit with all creation and let go of categories and abstractions, *duh*. So you don't so much mind standing in line at the bank for a few minutes to deposit your paycheck. Also banned: the phrases 'save your bacon,' 'out of the frying pan and into the fire,' and 'how the sausage is made,' which (to put things into perspective for you) are the dead baby jokes, Holocaust jokes, and Helen Keller rape jokes of waterpig world. Try, for once, to keep things tasteful.

Short world.

Here at last, in this here world finally of all possible, this blasted blacksmoke world, their respective pasts in all their unrecoverable pastness were rejoined. The sundering had been carried out by agents of the allfathers fully twenty years prior on Io, inside the gigantic perfectly spherical Inquiry Hall with its dozen entrances and but one exit. Those were bad times on Io, frightening, though as ever times were much much worse everywhere – worse still the farther you got from the seat of Inquiry. Four thousand dead policemen were reanimated to keep peace in one of the more...*libertarian* border systems. Several genengineered citizen-containment viruses saw limited official release, a blood parasite or two, on a more aggressive biocivics policy schedule than usual: among them the strain of DD1 Mattize that would later mutate into the so-called 'Laughing Fever.' The laws regarding memory-sundering were much more lax in those days, as the civil rights watchdogs and autonomous branch-populations (polyfathered, from the open-gensource exonucleic acid pools) hadn't yet found a sympathetic judge to start pushback from within the legal subsystem, while the 'trunk' population – the state-mandated, strictly source-controlled Good People – was very much enjoying its prosperity and catatonia, thank you, and so couldn't get worked up about a few undesirables losing a few undesirable memories. And in any case, how can someone genetically predisposed to criminality and subversion possibly give *informed consent* to a sundering? How could a margin-dweller understand the wide society's needs well enough to see the obvious necessity of his sacrifice...

Rexroth had been treated, at first, for traumatic childhood sex-abuse memories – standard – and a mild case of (doubtless somewhat related) misogyny stemming from early adolescent encounters with a blonde, a stone bitch no doubt; the technicians had signed off on the 60-day checkup results, All Clear, and he'd been freed up to return to work as a **Quality Assurance Technician, Sixth Form** on the redoubtable *AFS Imago*, best-known ship in the Io Perimeter Fleet. A small behavioural anomaly had turned up on his end-of-year workplace progress report, and per civil-service employment protocols Rexroth was called in for a routine memory rescan, which yielded a two-sided surprise: first, Rexroth was one of the Thousand, the remaining descendants of the first worker strain now prized for their mild precognitive abilities, and second, this species-strain-character – which should have manifested during adolescence – had been effectively suppressed for fully 26 years, and had only been exposed to his own cognitive monitoring routines by the sundering of the molestation memory. The techs found the whole situation – the surprise discovery of the species-character and their subsequent firing from the sundering facility – whole light years beyond annoying, though of course they were legally enjoined from commenting on such matters, even amongst themselves, for a period of 20 Io years. After all, humans had been molesting each other's kids since they first crawled out of the Sea, and they'd done just fine up 'til now, *great* really; that's where art came from after all; so why couldn't this chucklehead have just kept an angsty diary or done unnaturally dense-black oil paintings and just *lived with it* instead of popping open this can of genetic worms...

The allfathers' government now faced an interesting conundrum. Of the Thousand, only about sixty were still alive, and most of those were *non compos mentis* to say the least. Rexroth appeared to be perfectly healthy – indeed, now that he had dealth with his buried but dangerous and debilitating traumatic memories of molestation (pardon me, *now that it had never actually happened*) he was a model citizen and federal employee, he'd even taken up carpentry as a harmless pastime – and might now offer insight into the nature of the human precognitive faculty.

On the other hand, Rexroth's parents were stubborn and (oh by the way) unimaginably wealthy, planet-swallowing wealth I mean; and well-connected enough on the holonet that the standard black-ops extraction/isolation procedures might not go so smoothly. The allfathers were desperate to figure out the precogs' secret, but they were also pretty enthusiastic about keeping their jobs and their heads…

A four-year plan of behaviour modification and eventual incarceration (for the triple homicide which his state-mandated prescription medications would, over the course of those four years, subtly and inevitably compel him to commit) was settled on and put into practice; and Rexroth did indeed get around to bloodily/handily offing his thieving boss and two abusive coworkers, a full year ahead of schedule in fact – leading one of the allfathers to ask, *presciently,* whether Rexroth mightn't have known what was going on with the medications. Hmm. Naturally his parents couldn't object to him being taken into custody, and Rexroth was brought back to Io, to the Inquiry Hall, for the single most consequential interrogation in its history. It was there that his powers manifested fully, at last. Rexroth revealed to the allfathers that another of the Thousand (of the sixty!) was working right there in their midst, an allfather herself; and an emergency sundering was carried out on site, in the Inquiry Hall itself – both Rexroth and allfather Card in the sundering chamber at once, a hurried decision on the other allfathers' part; *a mistake* – ending in the catastrophic release of neuromagnetic energy which shattered the 4-steel structure of the Hall itself and laid waste to the great metal exoskeletons of Io.

The twenty years that followed were, as some apocryphal Chinese wit once said, *interesting*.

Rexroth and Card met again on the surface of Io after the war, on that there world finally, of all the many they had separately visited during two decades of what seemed, even to reasonable people, to be the death throes of the inhabited galaxy itself; and the hidden link between them – which the dual sundering had uncovered or even (religious lunatics and occult pseudo-science types were occasionally heard to say) *created* – became clear. All was revealed.

But not to us.

High clear sky and a hot wind blowing across the face of literary cliché world.

Ambient world. Lots of conversation going on in restaurants and cafes, never quite loud enough to disturb your thinking or writing, always just a hush or burble of sound to accompany Your Special Thing. All the light soft and flattering. No trouble reading even at night – there's always some nearby light source, even in pitch darkness, by which you can see just just just fine. And the dark itself is like linen or cotton balls. Close in: not the weird feeling of the *presence* of *distance,* but instead a reassuring pressure against your arm, or calming brush of shirtsleeve against your arm. The kind of dark you float in.

The TV is always on but never too loud, and when you catch a movie it's always just at the end of Act One, right before things go totally haywire, when you can still tell what's happening and get a sense for the stakes without needing to know details of the protagonist's Plan or have seen the black and white flashback scenes where we find out that during his childhood in Ireland he was beaten by Father O'Flaherty or what have you.

All the kitchens smell of fresh food, even when they're clean. Even the streets smell like fresh-baked bread.

The music lacks *oomph*.

Drumbeats ripple the skin of the awakening world. Flocks of mighty predator birds rise up screeching into daylight. Ocean surfaces heave up and crash, foam sprays hundreds of feet into the air. Small creatures skitter about nervously in damp hollows and caves. Bioluminescent lizards give off warning pulses and begin to move purposefully in precise geometric patterns, their tongues flicking to taste cavern dew; they hiss out protective incantations. Thousand-pound bullfrogs squat in their foetor below massive greybeard trees, slowly digesting the bodies of nearby village children whose mothers have long since given up the search. They quiver slighty in time to the earth's wavelike upwellings, and feel no anxiety, only a heightened awareness of the likelihood of their own deaths, like moisture sucked suddenly out of the air by a nearby gout of flame. Horses roll their eyes and spit foam flecks from the corners of their mouths as the madness comes on.

Stones crack, their inner structures melting and flowing into new, unnatural local sediments; the world's transformation is recorded in the sifting of dirt at the bottom of the ocean, the bodies it uncovers, patterns of thermal expansion and contraction which some visitor will read, millions of years later, with puzzled awe.

The queen was not expected to arrive so soon.

Her periodic eclipse and subsequent yearlong waning of power occurred during one of her many journeys to the outer dark; the idea that she might return *during* that time, risk stellar transit in her weakened state in full view of the hateful red eye itself, hadn't occurred to any living thing. Surely there would be another year of peace, one more at least. But she has returned *at the height of the occultation,* her light having dimmed sufficiently to be (painfully) visible to the naked eye, the clear blood in her veins no longer moving at all. Her mighty heart beating just once a day. Her skin is ashes.

This is unprecedented, or so the more conversational creatures releate to anyone who'll listen. Returned from the Black Fastness without benefit of her might? Impossible. Unprecedented! But while there is nothing to compare it to now, it has happened before. A thousand years ago, long past living memory. (Only the coral reefs can remember that far back, and they hold their tongues now, from prudence hard-learned.)

She is dying again.

She will steal one more innocent life, at terrible cost, and stretch it across the dwindling span of time until it becomes nervewracking, perilously thin – perhaps another thousand years – at which point she will die for the last time.

A single smooth blue hillside stone quivers. It is the only innocent being left in the whole world. It knows it is to be the sacrifice. Its agony will be great. The suffering of a stone lasts unbearably long, like life. She'll draw sustenance from the torturous transformation; but no pleasure. It is to be the old ritual again, the very oldest in fact: clawed hands pressed together in what might be sympathy, she will simply squeeze, and all order will collapse within it, dissipate hissing; the subatoms which become the stone will oscillate and flow, wildly at first and then with an almost fatalistic inevitability and calm, through every possible energy state and spatial configuration and intensity of information.

She gives to the stone the privilege of being part of her own Passage; and by a dark thermodynamic miracle she will be made new again. Crystalline. The ritual is one of the greatest, most terrible things in the universe: like dreaming of angels who descend to earth's surface bearing sunglobes to the dark places, leaving traces of dew on the grass where they step, singing with panflute voices, and stooping at intervals only to pluck out the eyes of curious children.

The stone will live out the history of every possible world, each in turn; it will become a catalogue of possible endings, collapsing gently into the one, the zero point: no order, no *being* will remain, only entropic *flux*. It will be unmade perfect.

The queen will feel every instant of this process, every fluctuation or flutter, every particle's sundering and irreversible dissolution. She will suffer with the stone; indeed she will be the nature of the suffering herself. At the zero point – or rather the infinity – she will enter, as she has once before, a state of blissful rapture, hands forced wide apart by a desire for endless welcoming. Her body will be perfectly still; and

oh

for a moment she will be the unmoving, unliving center of all universes, the fixed point. She will feel the stars wheeling about her feet, and light growing old as it turns into time.

To have this moment of perfection again she would murder an entire world. She would hate herself beyond the capacity of the world 'hate,' would spend lifetimes begging forgiveness; but the temptation is great. She knows. That's why the queen, of course: her will to knowledge surpasses all other earthly forces.

That's why she will allow herself, after one more restoration and occultation, to truly die.

❤ ☞ ✤ ☞ ✻

from 'R.T. Hamilton's *Dead Air*, a preliminary consideration': from *The World of All Texts, the Text of All Worlds* by L.P.R. Dodgson

Dead Air is the final volume of Roger Hamilton's 'Company of Men' quartet, and concludes Hamilton's ambitious experiments with classical narrative unities (and distinctly nonclassical voice) in suitably ironic-triumphant fashion. Like *New Wave, Old World*, and *Live Sound, Dead Air* takes place over the course of a single day – indeed, the present-time narrative occupies just a single hour – and its narrative is the first of the series to sport a 'happy ending' (however qualified and ambiguous, and despite the fact that it's the first event in the book, chronologically!). But *Dead Air* turns the quartet's structural formula on its end, extending the interpolated mini-narratives of *Live Sound* into analeptic movements of fractal complexity. The story of Fred Pleasant, the increasingly dissociative tax attorney, occupies a full 80 pages, but Pleasant appears only for an instant in the present-time frame narrative; Hamilton links Pleasant's story to nearly every other character's through coincidence (his wife cheats on him with Hawksmoor) or in conceptual terms (Pleasant's story darkly mirrors the tale of Mira's recovery and enlightenment after her 'accident'), but the attorney is just one of several characters whose connection to the book's ostensible center is tenuous at best.

And while *Dead Air* ends with contemplative silence – a welcome relief after the polyphonic rush of the previous 320 pages – the ominous title, which refers to *unwanted* or unwelcome quiet from a radio, indicates that the restful quiet of the subway car is both momentary and illusory. But Hamilton has set his final volume in the moments before the opening scene of *New Wave*: though the subway accident is mentioned only in passing in that first volume, we know that *Dead Air* is in fact a kind of prologue to the entire series, the missing human dimension to the black-comic media narrative of *New Wave*.

The complexity of the series's organization is even greater than that, though: just as *New Wave* and *Old World* overlap, as do *Old World* and *Live Sound*, that volume overlaps in turn with this one – and when the timelines are aligned, it's clear that not only do the four books tell a single story, they in fact tell four versions of the story of *the same day*. Mira and Raskin see the same plane take off; Pleasant and Hawksmoor separately eat at Mira's restaurant just moments before the fire; Curly never learns that his benefactor is the ghostly Bad Daddy; the concert that is *Live Sound*'s narrative center is the eventual destination of the school bus that leaves Pete Ramsbottom so distressed in *Old World*.

The series's titular 'company of men,' in other worlds, is linked both by Hamilton's storytelling and by those stories' shared 'reality' – the same reality that Hamilton goes to such lengths to problematize, seeming to reject it altogether in *Dead Air*. From that volume, here's Pleasant:

> The light the light but what if youre a trick of it. ohyeah!I know But seriously what if you. are. the light. Having a laugh. Laughing. Youre not real unless I say so I mean if I swear I will always believe I will hold you in place hold you up and then even then but its the light carries my words to you. Only where???do they go if youre not there first. Before me I need you to be here to hear me so I can be here to speak but if Im not here at all Mira Im saying you are beautiful as a new universe but you know why Im afraid.

And Hawksmoor:

> no but every language is constraint. yes but every language is pattern which is expansion. pattern multiplies what it orders; pattern is collision. you think you are repeating as if an old idea. no but you are yes, you yes are, yes you are singing the oldest song. magical is taking up old songs as responsibilities laid by. merely to allways be everything. please it is only chance. there is no shame in a universe in which all things are all things and nothing can be held against anything because everything being is allways acting. the one thing that can fill up the universe and deny nothing is Song.

And Mira:

> The smallness of it is OK. The bigness is OK. Closer listen for the news is bad; I mean 'news' is bad: it's not new. What's coming is the same what's come, probably. Tuesday a building was knocked over, I mean everyone in it died, and Wednesday night we went dancing…

The interior thematic connection or involution is intended to ground *Dead Air*'s imagistic play in a persistent reality – a thought-world, or feeling-world, if you like – an emotional effect which Hamilton, despite the critical regard for his later novels, never actually duplicated. And which was *not*, as we (of course) know, enough to catch the eye of the book-buying public.

♥ ☞ ✲ ☞ ✼

Worlding into being musicwise, I mean to say. A space is made btween two successive beat drops or breaks in silence, I mean to say, I mean there is a colour that sound has when you get close enough. It skims then breaks the plane of the skin. Projected line appears when arc of notes A B C# bends breathwise across the body, I mean to say, up over and into the curvilinear listening-space of you. Over into your own body. Space of rhythmic possibility opens up in place of solid bone, fibrous muscles reaching to complete wall shape...

Black bottomless drum shape appears. Thudder of bass billows drum now, or snap snare quick as gold glinting. Grey to white the snare now is. Trumpets yellow as you'd expect – did you learn to see them that way within you after light flashed off bell horn in lightspace or are there physical concordances even to your synaesthesia? – and clarinets wooden brown, bend blending as notes murmur into bass register winestained burgundy colours. I mean to sing what I see, look at the sound: wash of rotating search light for synth sounds come pianistic plink percuss even, unsteady now, sine waves too sinuous for mere mechanism. Analog synths plashed wet at mountain skin and up rose reaching treefingers in those places. Up they come grasping with leafprint patterns where mere human fingers go. To take, take, take root.

Or steelstring piano, sinew, old as the sounds which swirled before the form of music coalesced, ivory keys: I see you glassine, moving toothlike grind against antiparallel upper surface, clip quick skim keystroke surface, I hear Evans at the moment the river overbears greenbrown banks, I hear dead yellowed hands carouse, new architecture fluoresces into sound, dry possibility of one day a mathematics of sexuality in form on eday of *this* sound upon *this* skin. Long before the before we can now remember, even.

At world's beginning the first formless swell, whole tone sustain clustered without intention, giving over to the ice acoustics of dark space; and the first inkling of bodily life is dark trembling notes giving over (choke back tears but tears fall always, always, into everything away) to

    rest,

the break in formlessness – a physical thing, space is – which becomes form. The structure of any experience begins with absence; which we then fill by becoming. Entropy is nature's abhorrence of a vacuum. (Or I mean to say, nothing is as intolerable as a gradient, an imbalance – not tension, deep asymmetry. Inequality of opportunity is an unstable microstate.)

The bandeoneón, heartbroken, shimmers across curtain of warm air. Floor tap of heel. Something is coming into being. Skitter of melody at treble apex, tremble, tumble into midrange to be joined by unison guitar, clean sound of palmed strings unpicked, mourn of violin weeping within the moving microworld, fingertip-focus perception. Hot wind traces curlicue kiss across fertile pampas surface, earth skin: and then,

oh,

hearbreak, to surrender wearily to the sea. Salvation. Minor chord colouration, nocturne, cool air murmurs from noble range's recline; a city flares up, excrescent concentrate, an intensity of gridded crosshatch line, footsteps pizzicato countering machine hum of taxi cabs (present at the birth of the world, engine belch drowning baby world's birth wail). *They are dancing there.* Smell the sea. Or sense the suddenness of skin, left hand upon right hip, close catch: enough space between you for a world of sinful notion to arrive at its birth right here, dancefloor world, her toe point trace sweeping a wide circle across the parquet floor – arrested in *barrida,* gentle now, but now firm, yes, *there* – and she extends her leg to step so lightly (impossibly light her pure movement, she Weaves within the space of his embrace, his spine's straight line tangent as she curves, oh, *near*) across the space they share, movement flowers into the variegating walking cadence of a *molinete,* gaining speed, whirling closer, he wishes the skin of her face to touch his, to speak to him, her breath to move *through* him…

Meanwhile other worlds take their topology from other energies' upheaval, coalescence, collapse…Forty thousand children give over to ecstasy as guitar (or its electrical projection; the abandon and skitter of her fingers across taut steel string, Woven, comes into being at cables' distance only as shadow or notion; it is the *Sound* they crave, they follow, push and magnetic pull of signals at wired remove from the flesh in which they were firstborn, but while she can feel the music, its fullness as Act, she can no longer in this strange age touch the Sound) *breeeeeeeeaks* keening into a wail that isn't triumph, quite, unless death is. (Is it?) It isn't healthy. Dirt in the sound, injury. Years of accumulated invisibility and slow soul-deformation despite good intentions or spirits. Not your blues. The sound of a creature devouring its own heart to live, dying in the attempt.

The children sigh, batter their hands and feet on the ground, pantomime wracked dissolution. The end. The world is fully made. It's theirs. They know a sound that goes by suffering's name but they need never suffer. Not in this world that is theirs to dispose of. No loss, no death. They only hear music; it can never dissolve them. I mean to say they don't get to be unmade like we are.

Look look a world consisting mostly of naked folks getting all naked on each other's naked stuff all up in here. Some of them are even super good looking. In terms of the level of wonder and awesome it's like being a kid again only at the bottom of the pile of everything that is the world there's a hint of sadness because deep down no matter how fucked you get you can't ever get fucked enough to not be *here*.

'LET ME TELL YOU ABOUT MY COLLEGE FRATERNITY'

We were young and the world was ours, and it moved freely within another larger world we could not see; we had made of ourselves a world, a closed body consuming itself, littling bit by bit. It bore us across a great gulf whose horrifying immensity we would never speak of nor acknowledge, whose name was Time – *the world was ours* and we were the world, utterly Self-possessed, down to the private names we gave one another, which encoded our pairwise meanings, what we took to be our natures. We were idiots. I say we were blissfully happy, and scared, and our wonder at the things we found we could make was limitless. Discovery never seemed to cease. So many things fell into our laps or irrupted into our dreams seemingly out of nowhere for the millionth billionth time in the history of our species; dreaming creatures in deep sea caves called to us, blackly fluorescing, promising…their names were Time, as well. Time and its end…

Xenophiles all of us, or so we thought; but in such a small world, a traveling microworld (each of us kings of infinite space, right?), there was nothing new enough. Always hungry and we drove on hunting. Occasionally stopping to devour one another, brotherly, to become sustenance or demand it. We wanted the world to be as Strange as we felt. We read about lonely wanderers in far-off lands; we'd wept in every corner of our own tiny universe by then and dreamed of another. We imagined new forms that bodies might take, demihumans and tentacled horrors, which made our own mild deformities (or misperceptions) seem benign, even comforting. We spoke a private language so that any overhearing neighbour or creature or god would have the experience of alienness to which we were daily subjected by ourselves, our peers, dead ideas, fallen statues, ruins: hoping any visitor would play for us the part of the curious extraterrestrial, and we'd take turns being the leader it demanded to be taken to.

We assumed we would run into women in bearskin bikinis, for some reason, and they would rescue us from ravening beasts, and be pliant when making love among wild trees.

So young we would never die and the world was us. Sex seemed important, as a proxy for a coming intimacy which we couldn't yet put a language to. Women and men came and went. Such closeness but we weren't sure what we were close to – or couldn't say, or wouldn't. Each new passenger changed the complexion of the world-ship, altered its course subtly. We would demand to be untouchable but the stars simply glided past, unconcerned; or hot lava spouted from a hellfire sea beneath us, red yellow glowing globules liquid heat bursting all around, and inside the world-ship soft music played and someone insisted that the temperature drop another degree to 71 Fahrenheit, so we could sleep with blankets on. You would get lost in your partner's imperfections, stretch soul and body to accommodate them, and then slowly but surely abandon that new form when the next thing came up or around.

(Do you remember she used to lie about small things, or could never come with you touching her, or she worried so much about your happiness so she would never fall into the indulgent solipsism of being happy herself?)

(Do you remember he would get angry about the possibility of things, or fearful, and couldn't tolerate gentle kisses – only possession and rebuke?)

Bodies don't lie.

Our world-ship never ever did land. No 'safe passage,' no destination. Its skin simply thinned out, little by little, the stars growing brighter and their questions harder to escape, the noise of enveloping worlds biggening to a roar, until – one night while we all slept, or one day when our backs were turned – it vanished, leaving us afloat (as we had always been) with only one another's gravity holding our motley crew in place (as we had always known).

In time, that faded too.

Without a planet's surface to hold you, there is no up or down. Just floating. Just on and on.

We promised to stay young for one another, you *liar*.

❤ ☞ ♣ ☞ ✳

Graveyard world of old selves. They become playthings for the new self, or building materials: yeah that's the ticket: scattered mileposts gathered up and made into, say, pillars. Studs in the wall of the self every 18 inches or so. Bits of drywall. Paperback books, carefully matched in size, Krazy-Glued together to prop up a fading conception of, say, the kind of Artist you always thought you had it in you to be. A rigid plastic piece that keeps upright and undamaged by rampaging toddlers the gigantic impulse purchase that is the HD television known as the sexual identity, which broadcasts day in and day out without being able to produce anywhere near 24 hours a day of content. The libido really finds it audience (you) in reruns.

In the house of the soul everything is made of other houses. Dad wanted you to be brave but he didn't know how to be it himself, how to teach you that exotic thing; so instead he made you *effective,* and not knowing the difference (plus being, after all, well trained for it) you just got better and better at being perfectly adequate, *yay!* Your bosses love you but your husbands and wives see right through you and leave sooner or later. The messier and style-sloppier *they* are, the longer they stick around begging for you to fix *them*. Now you're in the middle (as usual) of refashioning yourself, and you still have only a kind of half-baked idea of what 'bravery' is.

You mistake carelessness for courage.

And so here you are, say, rock climbing without support ropes, or picking fights in the streets of Some Exotic and Dangerous Third World City Where Everyone Is a Knife-Wielding Criminal. You suppose that the bravest thing you could do is leave your older selves behind and become Bravery itself. It seems, in fact, that you'd like to be close to failure, even (especially!) to *dying* from your mistakes, when you make them. As if the bravest thing you could do is die smiling.

♥ ☞ ♣ ☞ ✶

A tour through the world of Lukacs Labs, a/k/a 'Mythos Labs':

ELI PONTY

Lukacs Labs got its start in the mid–1950's in a warehouse space rented by Eli Ponty, a chemical engineer and part-time inventor from Baton Rouge who remained in Boston after completing his PhD at MIT. Ponty's dissertation was careful research in polymers for industrial applications, but he focused his post-grad energies on independent research into self-regenerating chemical cycles. Ponty's quixotic interest in 'the atomic unit (forgive the dreadful pun) of universal *intention*' led him away from academia and won him a reputation as brilliant but hopeless – a *crank*, a great loss to academia. Ponty spent two years in the Himalayas in the early 60's, but never spoke of his activities there; he returned to Boston in peak physical shape and immediately started putting together an odd research laboratory – staffing his warehouse building with a motley crew of engineers, scientists, explorers, mapmakers, outsider artists, even literary critics. Within a year he had 66 full-time employees. His new hires came and went at odd hours; many or most simply moved into the building, which he allegedly purchased outright on the day he returned from Asia.

In the 70's Lukacs Labs was the best-known loft space and hangout venue in Boston, and though a notorious 1972 drug raid turned up nothing, the firm's central role in the national LSD network was tacitly understood by all involved; in the 80's Ponty's advocacy of the complete abolition of copyright law garnered unwanted, very visible attention from the government, though he and his lab had been the the subject of ongoing federal inquiry since the late 60's. Ponty's name was attached to a number of spectacular Internet IPOs during the Clinton administration, and he provided angel startup funds for Google (the spectacular returns on which continue to fund the Labs' 21st-century operations).

Ponty is rarely seen in public, though he's not a recluse. He and his wife Marie-Ann live in one of the Lukacs Labs warehouses – the Labs occupy three adjoining waterfront buildings in Boston, a decommissioned military base in Oakland, and an unknown number of properties elsewhere – and occasionally go out in Boston and Cambridge. But Eli maintains a curious air even on social occasions: the novelist Adam Bray once described seeing Ponty 'staring glassily into space like Santa Claus on Boxing Day,'

> as if the holographic perspective afforded by visiting every child in every earthly human settlement had overwhelmed his direct experience of mere objects. What might otherwise have been life had been reduced to an interval between such moments of exhaustive and exhausting vision – and worse,

there was no one to commiserate with but God, and Santa Claus doesn't have the luxury of believing in imaginary beings other than himself.

Bray is not a well-regarded novelist by any means, but Ponty has praised that book for its 'matter-of-factness.' He turned 80 this year; it is a mistake to see him as old. Indeed his so-called 'biological age' has, since at least 1962, been most precisely described as 'indeterminate.'

ANTHONY (TONY) HEAP

Eli Ponty's first hire upon returning from the Himalayas was Anthony Heap, a painter and cartographer from a suburb Philadelphia. In 1961, at age 17, Heap achieved brief, minor recognition for an exhibition of his work at a Philadelphia gallery. The paintings showed astonishing care and craftsmanship, but were difficult to categorize, and therefore critical failures. Each painting was a meticulously hand-drawn map of some distant country, 'marred' by a surreal insertion or interpellation: a geometric cluster of nonexistent cities, an imaginary symmetrical mountain range, notes from a fictional explorer's journal, or a river system flowing in impossible mathematically-precise spiral patterns around a fictional stone circle.

Heap's mother Natalie was herself a trained draughtsman and the only woman in the Earth Science department at DePaul University, but claimed she played no part in the production of the paintings. Tony Heap insisted otherwise; he claimed to have drawn inspiration not from his own dreams but from his mother's – and her mother's, and hers...This was written off as a charming affectation by the gallery show attendees, disdained as either Oedipal creepiness or barely-suppressed homosexual identification by the folks in Heap's hometown.

Ponty specifically cited both the strange maps and Anthony's purported inspiration when he offered Heap a job in summer 1963. Heap had matriculated at DePaul to take advantage of the reduced tuition afforded by his mother's employment there, but he immediately accepted Ponty's offer of a research grant in 'speculative cartography' and moved to Boston; the generous terms of the grant placated his parents while the bohemian living conditions and Ponty's serene conviction appealed to Anthony himself.

Now 65 years old, Anthony Heap has produced more than two thousand maps in his lifetime, a feat which would baffle his colleagues in the art world if any of them had the slightest idea. His work is occasionally shown in 'outsider art' exhibitions, but he remains largely unknown despite his peerless and allegedly untutored technical facility. One painting is a 20'x20' photorealistic image of a settlement in south Wales which (Heap insists) existed 15,000 years ago – long before anything resembling a human being was known to live in Wales. No respectable scholar takes this assertion seriously; fortunately Lukacs Labs employs a team of less-than-respectable anthropologists, at least one of whom (Andrew Greenstreet) claims to have found physical traces of the settlement depicted in Heap's painting. As the Labs' employees are known for interdisciplinary collaboration and a boozily pranksterish sense of humour, no scholar takes this assertion seriously either.

Greenstreet recently received a grant from the University of Cardiff, and has not been heard from in two months; he was last seen entering Heap's studio in the Labs' original waterfront building.

VASILY KIRKOV

As a 25-year-old computational biology postdoc Kirkov won notoriety last year for his claim, in a footnote to an otherwise well-regarded and uncontroversial *Science* article, that the 'human rights' framework would be abandoned by 2025 as the concept of the 'human' was stripped of both legal utility and scientific meaning. Kirkov had made a splash his rapidly-developing field when, after earning his PhD at Harvard at age 23, he turned down tenure-track offers at a half-dozen universities to stay on as a poorly-paid postdoc in his Cambridge lab; his cryptic 'human rights' remark further depressed his career prospects, as did his erratic behaviour at conferences and seminars.

Of course, Kirkov could afford such irresponsibility; he'd been safely employed by Lukacs Labs since age 16 anyhow.

Vasily works in a small but well-equipped computer lab in the main waterfront building. He regularly disappears into his office for a week at a time, only emerging to carry on about (recently) the telic inauthenticity of 'evolution' as a biological paradigm, the meaninglessness of 'life' as a category, and the upcoming digital/informational recapitulation of the transition from the primordial 'RNA world' to the contemporary 'DNA world.' Kirkov displays a kind of cheerful disdain toward most of his colleagues at Lukacs Labs, though his more emotionally-intelligent labmates recognize this as a defensive posture and perverse form of social outreach.

Though he lacks Eli Ponty's capacity for cross-cultural conversation, Vasily Kirkov worships the old man – and they frequently spend hours and hours arguing in Vasily's lab about every topic under the sun (and a few from beyond it). The two men share a passion for space opera, though Kirkov has never confessed to Ponty that at age 11 he wrote a text-based virtual reality system based on a midcentury pulp novel that Ponty himself had recommended offhandedly in a 1976 newspaper interview. What Kirkov doesn't know, meanwhile, is that Ponty is already aware of this private homage – and owns the online storage company that hosted the system in the mid–90's.

This is a coincidence, of course – along with, as Kirkov would put it, 'every bit of nothing that's ever not really happened.' He's actually a fun guy when you get to know him.

KENNETH GROVE

Ken is a 35-year-old hardware hacker from Colorado who built physical systems for ubiquitous gaming and ARG's (Augmented Reality Games) before coming to Lukacs Labs four years ago at Ponty's request to work on sustainable computing technologies. He does still work on games systems though – indeed, Grove is responsible for an unannounced (and thoroughly inscrutable) gaming project that involves placing 15,000 low-cost matchbook-sized electronic devices throughout the city of Los Angeles – hidden in fake plastic rocks, attached to the tops of streetlights, hot-glued to the undersides of manholes, even embedded in the sidings of new downtown office buildings. The devices' purpose is unknown; they have no visible power source, physical sensors, or transmission circuitry.

Ken has a knack for keeping secrets; before his expulsion from Carnegie Mellon he designed and ran an infamous weeklong campus-wide ARG that combined scavenger hunts, live-action roleplaying, a baroque variant of Capture the Flag, and steam-tunnel spelunking. Details of the game are hazy (and the campus police reports are maddeningly vague), but apparently it led to the temporary shutdown of CMU's computer network. The spelunking got him expelled, officially, but it also led to his job offer from Ponty, who admires Grove's rebel spirit.

Ken is one of LL's most personable researchers, an avid reader and collector of rogue engineering artifacts dating back a thousand years. He's incidentally responsible for the current best theory (submitted to *Nature* on a lark and quite unexpectedly published) of how the Maya fabricated the rubber materials for their infamous human-sacrificial ball game. He's also an enthusiastic but wildly inaccurate singer, which has never stopped him serenading his labmates, one of whom has received extensive operatic voice training but has the good grace to refrain from criticism. She secretly enjoys Ken's performances anyhow – rigid formality and emphasis on musical 'correctness' were the reasons she left the conservatory anyway.

FRED KAISER

About five years ago Kaiser became the public face and *de facto* showrunner at Lukacs Labs; a former CMU classmate of Ken Grove, he is a supernaturally committed mechanical engineer and nontraditional pedagogue, just 34 years old but already a millionaire ten times over (on his own account) from a teaching-toys line he developed in college. His new toy, *Gigaflop Megaflip* (*Flopflip* for short), is a programmable robot, toad shaped, able to emulate specific human voices in a wide variety of emotional dispositions with an accuracy variously described as wondrous, nightmarish, and – in the worlds of his dissertation advisor – 'impossible given today's technology, absolutely fucking impossible...and yet there it is. Terrible name though.'

Fred shares living space in one of LL's waterfront buildings with Ken Grove and both their wives, who run a decidedly non-traditional engineering-centric grade school in Boston's South End, where some of the Labs' less dangerous projects receive their first public trials. Fred and Ken collaborated on *Flopflip* last year, though Grove insists his contribution was of the late-night bull-session variety. Kaiser is a devotee of post-Singularity science fiction, Wagnerian opera, and Middle Eastern cuisine; he and his wife are fanatical monogamists, though both have learned over the last half-decade to be tolerant of the libertinism that serves as a kind of scarily high-energy social glue in the Labs.

Fred and his wife have four of Tony Heap's paintings hanging in their bedroom; they optimize their personal finances and household maintenance tasks with a singlemindedness that borders on the supernatural. The key to the Labs' culture (and the Kaisers' place in it) lies somewhere between those two poles of whimsical surrealism and maniacal pursuit of knowledge.

You might say the work of the Labs is the maniacal pursuit of whimsy: *intense play.*

❤ ☞ ✣ ☞ ✳

> *Fur is big. Mud is big. The stick is big. The word is big. Fire is huge. The wheel is huge. The line and circle are big. On the wall, the line and circle are huge. On the wall, the man at the wall makes a man from the circle and line. The man at the wall makes a Word on the wall from the circle and line. The Word on the wall hears my Father.*

Text's innerworld.

Its secret function. Private logic, preconscious. Its secret.

So often looking into the self is an act of imposition. The interpretive faculty begins to spin out a heavy fabric, occluding.

We won't welcome ourselves to see. The symbol-set is there to provide a scaffold for speech; it substitutes for intention. Water doesn't *want to* flow downhill but it has tendencies. Such a thing as universal inevitability. Perhaps I mean narrative flow. The symbols permit us to become flow. Overflowing cups, falling bodies, a sigil engraved on a table.

Or there is a story there. Or we are a story there. We storymake ourselves into the circular family of symbols, simple. We so much want to be coherent. (*Is this making sense?* in a plaintive voice.) (I mean does it feel like a Catalogue or does it list things you can buy like a Story.)

No secret but us. We come to the world of words to be revealed.

But we can not see a circle sitting atop a line without interpolating (imposing) our own form. We symbol-see, and so strip the symbols of their deeper occult power. They could show us ourselves, could we allow it; but we mirror merely: and are satisfied with naming the symbols we see. The Usurper. The Father. The Empty Table. The City. The Dead.

Taking attention away from the self-sight we came looking for; and so it goes, and so we go on, so this is how we go on after all. After all the life is done.

There should be a revealed logic but we reject the possibility that there is something we don't *already* see. We don't want to be caught rocked back on our heels, unstable.

Up-is-down-ism. So you can't have fallen flat, no. You're floating on your back. No ground, I figure.

We wish all of us to be transformed, to flow together. *To become one another.* That would be bliss; or heaven. What we wish when we say 'heaven' and what we mean, and what we wish we meant, and what the worlds say, and what countermelody courses below or against them. (*point counter to stutter rhythm of speech that halts in the throat glottal becoming ugh cch hk now breath airword and hisper anew, no, yes now, steady, sweet slow now, to be born our mouths in your mouth*)

But allbeing-unto-nothingness catches in the throat. I mean you have to be careful who you become into. The idea of you has to maintain the idea of no. It has nothing else left.

The text should take us there. The words. Circle and line on the wall could be. The cards could be. Her upturned mouth could be. Winter mouth opening alleyway cold could be. The crumble of heaven. Empty buildings transitive. Strange visions could. Steel his thighs machinic warm weight upon you belly to belly could be. Transformed. We could be we. You could unmake me. Hand touches now mouth, tongue trace worry line or the line of life to come, **the many worlds of you which may be**, future comings, you ache, bodies think and feel, your unchaste mind is your unbent body, the cards are nothing, the symbols nothing, lines upon the body only lines, *the body breathes…*

Gotta unmake ourselves. To want to want: to know all the words we may yet visit, spread waiting upon shadow carpet stained with starlight. To want (I want us to) to know (all of us) what we know to (each becoming the body of) want (every other). I wish to *burst* within you. Would you contain me. Would you become me. I would want to dissolve.

Distance between any two worlds…

Would you (I) dispose of my thinking body.

Make of me a world

                      yes

Rock and roll world, PLAYED OUT! Oh, just *admit it*.

Mainstream Hollywood film world – OK, also played out, but before we get there let's *get into character* just the tiniest bit

— Mainstream Hollywood film world, to repeat, in which sex happens only to the young, it usually involves either violence or embarrassment, no one is kinky, thuggery is arousing, the English are Victorian prudes and fonts of worldly wisdom (also evil), no one is really really ugly, people with dark skin have magical powers to make people with light skin feel better (also **TERRORISM**), and there exists something called 'magic hour' right around sunset where the light is just perfect and everything really heart-tugging and/or dramatic happens then, invariably, making the afternoon commute in Los Angeles an absolutely surreal fucking nightmare. Oh, it's a mad mad mad mad world and, sidebar, old women are disgusting. Young women are nerds or whores. Nothing's as classy as a good-looking victim.

Eventually everyone will be one. ~~I mean a victim. No, a nerd.~~

WHORE!

Mocking all good sense: clown world.

World where the term 'feminism' never caught on; instead, activists for sexual equality call themselves *menarchists*. Bonus terrible pun: the song 'Menarche in the UK' is a counterculture hit. The world is poorly off.

There were ducks, for a while, in her dreamworld; but one morning upon waking she realized she'd copped them from a popular television show that aired when she was in high school, one of the few 'adult' activities she and her mother both enjoyed (though they watched the series at different times, of course), and though she made no conscious effort to un-duck her private dreamwise image-library, after that they didn't turn up to visit very often. Maybe memories wish to work in secret, giving off just a grey drear, just enough to work by in the brain's recesses, which daylight gracelessly obliterates.

She built up the geography of her dreams slowly. Their architecture. She had done some reading on 'memory palaces' in a class, years before, then forgotten ever doing so; but that was the right metaphor, or a right-enough one anyhow, for understanding the process.

There was a house, immensely large though not tall, its profile a bit like the tidal island Mont Saint-Michel. In fact it was basically that island entire, but big-house-sized, complete with miniature abbey on top, though she had no memory of ever having seen the place. Certainly she'd never visited. Her island-house dreamworld was filled with improbable subterranean tunnels, some lit by floating bioluminescent globes, some dark beyond the dark. A humming sound filled the tunnels. For a long time she couldn't think of where she'd seen the island.

She realized one morning, mulling over the historical and topological oddities surrounding (making?) her dreamworld, that she was under the impression that Mont Saint-Michel (she had by then turned up the name of the place, and was just noticing that her dreams were starting to get a bit less vivid, maybe as a result) housed not only an old old monastery but a Villa of some sort, small yellow and sunlit, beautiful, simple, where once upon a dangerous time the spear that pierced the side of Jesus was housed.

She'd read something about it once. The Spear. Oh for god's sake. It'd scared her half to death. While traveling through Europe on a bus tour with her family she'd struck up a friendship – which was, though she didn't understand why, in some ways unhealthy; or so her mother thought – with a childlike man from Skokie, Illinois. He'd responded to her interest in European history by lending her a lurid paperback book, Ravenscroft's *Spear of Destiny,* which promised the secret history of the Spear of

Longinus and (wait for it) the true cause of World War II, i.e. (wait for it) Hitler's mad quest for the Spear. She didn't process any of the Hitler balderdash at the time, though, because she was too tweaked by a series of odd coincidences to do with the trip: her mother's insistence on visiting the Hofsburg in Vienna, where the Spear (or a fake, per Ravenscroft) is supposedly displayed; the exciting tour stop on the Isle of Capri, where – she'd have sworn, it'd been so long since she read that ridiculous book – where the Spear was hidden for a time, maybe in the Temple to Tiberius(?!); the confusing references in the book to – (oh) – Mont Saint-Michel itself, which she always confused with Capri, still does actually, and which probably had nothing to do with the Spear, come to think of it, but which had lingered in her memory as a kind of shape-archetype, every once in a while simply skipping out of its memory-slot and into a place theretofore set aside for something altogether more mundane, like 'the idea of a house sitting on a hill' or 'hobbit town.'

Not that hobbits are mundane, not *here* anyway.

She'd snuck the Ravenscroft text into her travel bag – the little man's eyes had twinkled – and at night she'd read it in hungry bites of twenty, forty, eighty pages. No wonder she'd been too tired to pay much attention to the Euro-sights themselves.

Beneath the house, catacombs opened to her dreamsight like black mouths full of limestone teeth and cavewater pools crawling with unclean things. She saw the island-house in cutaway profile, as in the *Learn About History!* picture books she'd read as a child, with their colourful line drawings of schooners and castles. (There was a tiny figurine of a knight in a largeish castle, in a child's attic, and one day the knight came to life; and there was a coin with an unsmiling god's face on one side, but on the reverse of the coin he was smiling, she remembered suddenly,

~~and the smile was much much worse...~~

Lovely tree-lined parks unrolled from the house like the turf on her high school's soccer field being replaced over the summer. (~~She had volunteered to help out with the restoration at her guidance counselor's suggestion. 'Volunteerism looks great on the résumé,' Mrs Nuttall had said. Even then the idea seemed contemptible, like — where did this image come from? — doping up a child to keep it quiet.~~)

Her dreamworld *was* an island, it turned out. Though not Mont Saint-Michel after all. Ringed all around within sight of the house, not with water, but with a kind of roiling mist, like the tops of clouds whipped into fibrous wisps by (~~flying with him to be at his own father's funeral; he thought she was being callous but he couldn't understand she'd been through Death before, a couple of them too close and too too young, and she could see past the ending but he couldn't~~) an airplane's passage. Crystal creatures swam though the mist, and glass; their bodies lightly chimed as their spines flexed or heads rotated miraculously along three axes at once. There was no sky; or rather there were hundreds of skies, blue purple speckled clear pearled marbled and broken carelessly open, each contained in one compartment of what seemed to be a massive world-spanning bookshelf, upturned and kept (by a dream's cheeky answer to gravity) from scattering its celestia across the world like angel-children's toys.

A mountain in the distance: 'beyond' the sea of mists, though she could get there easily enough. Worlds are dreams after all, or versions of the same dream. The mountain's stone skin crawled with formless living things. Their scales glittered. She could see all their cells from afar. The sun welled up within the mountain like an underground lake, burbling to the surface, and poured over the rocks into the mist. Seconds ticked away audibly. Palm fronds and pine needles carpeted the valleys around the mountain. Rain rose. Huts toppled over, caught by wind, cataracted over cliff faces, and dissipated; rainbow spectra flashed where they fell. No one ever wept.

She could smell bread baking, books, her grandmother's apartment, petroleum tang. She heard musical surf. Unseen grass rustled, sheets on a sunstained backyard line billowed.

At times a kind of emotional dysmorphia would take her over and she wouldn't dream for several nights running, or would do so only in fits and starts, unable to sink deeply enough to find the blissful contiguity of being that alone could take her out of her body and into…everything else; or bring all other things into being with(in) her self, drift through the interstices of her thinking-body and populate her many private innerworlds. At those dislocated moments she could only return gingerly to her dream-self, tissues tearing (all birth is rebirth; no birth without pain; suffering is refusal), her bones and muscles a stumbling gangle. Conscious suddenly of the decided physicality of her dream-threshhold, the audible tick of conscious thought (ON) giving way (OFF) to the cover of inner dark.

There's nothing worse for a dreamer than self-consciousness.

Oh, and horses. Not winged, not since she was a girl. But free and unfettered. Chestnut mares at unworried saunter through knee-high sparse grass – there was grass, and a cave with talkative goblins – their foals dawdling nearby, gorgeous and uncertain.

One sky-cubbyhole would empty over a hidden grove; a dazzle of rain would spiral down, whirling; she would remember the first boss she really respected, or seeing four straight sunrises from the studio, or jigsaw puzzles with her cousins from Slingerlands when she was a girl; the warming sun would pry stones loose from the north wall of her night-house, and the echo of their fall would clatter on interior walls and through the catacombs, would return as a man's voice: her father's, Eric's who would never kiss her in front of his friends, or Mr Kinnaird's from the apartment down the hall, dead for nearly ten years but still good for a laugh.

Before they left, the ducks were prone to waddle around wobbly by the causeway (it couldn't possibly have been Mont Saint-Michel, but then where did the causeway come from?), quacking at distant cars, which never came all the way up to the house. Not only did the causeway separate her private world-house's inner body from whatever lay beyond the ring of mist, but the land-bridge itself was separated from the house by a stretch of thirty feet, or a hundred; too far to cross, even at a running jump! was the point. If dream-stuff has a 'point.'

Actually the ducks didn't leave, as such – they just stopped being there, bit by bit. Not invisiblizing or anything, no visual drama like hands (wings?) growing transparent while trying to play the guitar. They were just less and less a part of the dream-body, receding like pain, or pleasure. They vanished from the world of possible things long before she noticed that they were gone.

She was reminded, a few years down the line, that for all the ducks' importance on that damn TV show, they appeared only briefly, in the first episode – and were never seen again. Indeed that was the whole point of their inclusion in the narrative; they were always (but only) the thing that once beautifully was, or was to have been. Her mom would always talk about the ducks, how she hoped they'd come back at the end, maybe just in the final episode, to give Tony just that little bit of happiness or peace – even though she hated Tony.

She supposed that her mom wanted peace for herself, but wasn't willing to ask for it aloud. In any case they didn't come back, not even in the final episode. And she undreamt the ducks too, by noticing them. Each dreaming body is fragile, its geography a provision. (Y'know even the invisible beginning-beauty that spheres into the space between you'n'me.) The world is so easily unmade.

'Did you ever hear about this, Mom?' she asked.

'What's that, hon.'

'The Spear of Destiny. It's –'

'Is that one of those ridiculous occult books that Terry reads?' (Jesus, his name was *Terry*.) 'Honey, we *talked* about him…'

'What? *No.*'

'It is, isn't it. Tell me the truth.'

'It's *history,* Mom.'

'It's a load of garbage is what it is. Why don't you pay attention to what we're doing, for heaven's sake? Have you even noticed we're in the mountains?'

She hadn't, actually. Not that it mattered. There were other mountains, maybe more beautiful than these; there was even one just out beyond the swirl of mist, rising out of old ground like a remembered principle. Not just rock. And a sideways bookshelf sky ridiculous with light, its leaves opening, falling, every story's written line rich with new worlds; and not a cloud in any sky except as she dreamt it. She *knew* the story about the Spear was nonsense, is the thing. No one believed her but. She *knew* what was real and what wasn't, could see the stitches at the seam, skies disjoining each other; but knowing didn't give her joy. She and her Mom were just different people, was the thing. Her Dad always said so, which she'd hated him for and still kind of did. In the mountains she'd begun to see what he meant. *You come from different words,* was how he put it. Something like that – or that was the form the memory had taken, her memory (the Being she'd begun), by something much older and deeper than choice.

MAGIC CIRCLES

Gameworld or some third thing. Draw the widest possible circle first: *It matters. Things matter.* That'll do for a deep-down far-out operating fiction if you like. Rule 1 or 2 or so, There's more than this, more than 'more than we can see,' even. We can agree on that, with attendant obligations: act for the future, beyond-all-this has some intrinsic value, and so forth. Tiny little Earth on the ass-end of the outer spiral arm of the 'Milky Way' – already an interpretation. Add to the above: *Names matter.* We go be where they tell us. And of course some names carry a little more weight than others. Even in a maybe-infinite universe it's *the* Milky so-and-so, though you've got to think, floating out there with nothing to do *but* think (boring…), that no way are all the other Ways non-Milky in a universe a billion times bigger than the very idea of 'bigger than.' Every universe you can imagine can probably fit inside this one unless your imagination has or is some kind of superpower. OK, but let's agree to narrow our scope a little, the playing field: nice quick camera push in from the nearby zillions of swirling celestial bits'n'parts to just this rock, 'ours' (haha), fire in the middle and moist surface like a jalapeño cupcake; but in terms of playing equipment someone should keep an eye on the nearby big yellow fireball and dumpy little orbiting rock too, which'll come into play later probably – the sun is the game clock, for one thing.

Wait'll you feel what *injury time* looks like.

So there's *our* rock, the term for which is 'oblate spheroid' though doesn't it look like a ball, bouncing there along an arc so slow it looks like floating? Heck if you could see a basketball caught in strobelit time it's got that same shape, maybe some Jupiter-sized giant dribbled us a billion years ago on his-her-its way to an asteroid basket and is two steps away from the all-time most important *traveling violation* in the history of ever, ever. No visible lines. Huh. But still the play…

We didn't forget about you, float on by, closer: first funny thing from out here (unless you thought the cupcake thing was funny?) is the great watery space-rock doesn't look anything like the one on your teacher's desk, is distinctly *nondescript,* which is frustrating. How are you supposed to find 'Kazakhstan,' for instance, or 'Burma,' or 'Philadelphia'? (How also did you know that this space maps onto that?) Enter a low-earth orbit just outside the upper-atmospheric haze, whatever 'up' means, careful not to get to close else you'll surface-skip like a stone and end up ass-up out in the pitch-black of outer space, not that you're certain at this point that 'out' is the right world. The whole thing seems pretty 'out,' doesn't it. Plus what's 'black' again? So maybe we need to go back and pencil in that circle as well, assuming for the sake of argument a pencil big enough, plus also that our metaphor-universe is made of paper. Or I guess screen first then it was print. Or, no, back up and out ('out,' etc.) further and *Assume metaphor,* also *Assume 'You.'* Which covers the pencil/paper bit, I desperately hope, so pencil in another enormous circle labeled *Words stick.*

They don't change without you saying so. Though, again: boring.

On the other hand that should cut down on the parentheticals, I hope.

Look at that cloud brushing across where you're pretty sure 'Massachusetts' should be. Like a gigantic ungodly shower scrub. Wait, 'ungodly'? Leave it aside a moment. Meanwhile look at this border you're crossing, now: say a cloud is a thing unto itself and not, say, a region of increased density or local variation in affinity between molecules, which you've probably heard of but not seen. Easy to see from up here that there's a floating ocean *above* the celestial cupcake, bound to it by gravity (which points 'down,' sigh – play along, you're doing great), made of air. But agree not to see it, not as an 'it.' Stipulate – here's some insane fun for you, cosmonaut – a more or less empty 'sky,' give borders to the clouds (as if oceans were skies for fish to fly through, though who knows whether the fish see things that way, what game *they're* playing). Call them distinct things, and indifferent. Plus, yes, an 'ozone layer,' the atmosphere's end zone, pretend, which (though made of the same sea as the sky) *is*, contrastingwise, in our minds and most others' a single thing. Pretend it's sitting there still like a city 'waiting' to be bombed. But then we need gigantic air quotes for 'city' and are getting ahead of ourselves…

Beneath the roiling aboveground sea an assortment of shells, rocks piled, the crust and border of earth distended: stretched upward into shapes (just wait'll I tell you about 'shapes') and sizes distinguished not only by their own characters but by the meanings of the natures of the meanings we – no, somebody – layered on them. A structure of structures, unfortunately private, imaginary. Where we're gonna run into trouble here, you figure, is this whole thing where 'imaginary' doesn't mean 'not real.' Not quite. You, by the way, with your ridiculous 'Massachusetts' notion, ridiculous on face but making a kind of sense from the inside, compared to Texas or whatever: you're welcome to come screaming across the sky like a V–2 but if you get 'too' close to the ground, which in general b.t.w. you are *not* the judge of, there's a 'limit' to how fast you get to go. Not that anyone can make you stick to it. And if your feet scrape the ground you're a flying-thing landing, whatever 'landing' means – 'landing' is like separating one 'cloud' into two – but then flatten your soles against the top floor of earth 'within city limits,' Jesus this is complicated, and you're a pedestrian and can more or less go as fast as you want. *The rules don't scale up to walking at flight speed.* Wait though –

Welcome, incidentally, to 'America.' Your guess is as good as mine, and you have to guess.

There's a border to the city and we nod as we cross it. It doesn't extend up, exactly. Right? Draw an imperfect circle about the center of it though not the *actual* center, gold-domed round house in which the name and nature of the commonwealth inheres. 'State house.' Learn the nomenclature. (Oh, and gold matters here. Is that true where you read from? Is no one sane *anywhere?*)

The center of the territory is off to the right of the map, by the water, by the border. (Does the one ebb and flow with the other?) You're just gonna have to trust me. Or trust Them, more to the point. Or wait: I think I got those backward. The center of the map – not of space but of idea – I mean the most important square on the gameboard...aah the hell with it.

If by chance you miss the border on your way in you're still bound to it; others wait to bind you. While jaunting across the galaxy you acquired a certain admirable broadness of vision but it's time to surrender that, focus your eyes, resolve the brownian swirl of molecules – each a secret probabilistic cloud, essences discretized and permuted into a shape that can be every shape

– into, irritatingly, Bostonians. Some of them also 'Massholes' though that name comes and goes like a trump suit. Though c'mon, space traveler, and consider playability for a moment: really it's like all four players decide on their *own* trump suits and play to figure out who's who, who's even partnered with whom, North with West maybe. Yes we're passing over how there can be a 'north' on the surface of a great spacegoing basketball in oblate midbounce, who put the poles there, whether you actually know how to play bridge, why the speed limits are written in miles not radians, plus *kilometers* for the rest of the word. Hey, do they have trick-taking card games in 'outer' space, where you come from?

But then 'the rest of the whatever,' nation, family, whatever – all that rests on an entire set of circles we're not even arm's length from, and not just because 'arm's length' is always a ballpark figure to begin with. (So is 'ballpark,' as a Euro/Masshole meeting would quickly reveal.)

Whip-pan over here, please. No, *here!* To our destination, this 'apartment building.' **Where do we even *begin*.** Assume ownership, enforcement. Assume enforceability. Assume stable location while tacitly admitting (or postponing until junior year) quantum fluctuation, probably with a neato Not In My Probabilistic Field: flux for thee, not for…oh, well, assume a more or less stable 'me,' though that's even more quantum than quantum, honestly. As 'you' will see.

Play along with this street-naming scheme that is *fantastically* arbitrary and dumb, whatever 'streets' are – they're for cars, maybe? the space between boxes of rock and powder, glass-windowed? but only at this stage in the game, this go-round – and now bind yourself to something called 'contract law' which says among other things that you have to sign a contract to be stuck inside it but you didn't get to decide that rule, that power vests in someone else, elsewhere.

Your turn next. Pretend there's no flow of material, at every level, between the building and the therefrom-derived outside, and – oh yeah – as 'out' as outer space was, as homesick as you're probably feeling right now for Betelgeuse or Caprica or Tatooine or wherever home is (don't worry, you don't exactly have to know what 'home' means, though if you wear a hat you can conveniently hang it there) (or vice versa), outside-the-window is *just that out.* You don't get more or less 'out.' Dwell there a moment. Assume neighbours, but if you know what's good for you do not assume neighbourliness; in fact the opposite; fine, but then later on, when whoever's next door pisses you off playing his music too loud, you can call him out for breaking the circle you never really expected him to honour. Oh speaking of which: assume music. Assume, unfortunately, *pop* music. Distinguish between like a thousand genres of same, each subdivided by style, which if you're interested in being popular you're gonna need to memorize a few of them and develop a fondness for whichever few are appropriate right now. We'll tell you which those are later.

By the way: welcome to America, you're interested in being popular.

Wait outside the window a second. Listen to the music: music is to give meaning to feelings radiating out ('out'!) from whisper-thin hidden skin of our ears. Looks like jazz. Feel bad, incidentally, for being 'outside looking in,' notice that circle, wonder what it takes to permeate the membrane surrounding this place. The basically-a-cube became a bedroom when they slept in it. They 'slept together' there first. *Not* the same. They're…well, who knows what they are. *They* don't, even. The space became a 'room' when they took up residence here, scale of subdivision altered, the building's interstices reabstracted into rooms – there are rules for naming but everyone's forgotten them and everyone keeps following them. A well-worn groove in the earth is enough to make a track, a circle in the surface, where if you find yourself going fast it's 'racing,' inducement without intention, an invitation to others to *beat you* – it's a pain, really. So much of this is pain. They're close now (*relative to* bodily scale), horizontal (*relative to* etc.), 'she' and 'he' are. Coalesced into a pair. They are them. (Her clothes a declaration, his distinctly different, intersecting sets. Strewn about the room in a meaningless pattern. Which garments shed and which worn constitute some symbol set or setting.)

This is gonna be weird but I think we're gonna have to restart here, because this subgame has the power to modify the greater game maybe. To push the borders of this inner circle out, be the new Furthest Thing. Sorry, but: *Assume Us*. 'It matters' was hard enough but her hand rests on his cheek, close, offering, true, and she says to him now that 'That's all that matters.' Magic worlds again. Say she has something to give, something he and they can have; say her hand on his cheek is more precious than that same hand resting on his forearm or now any other thing, those static-standing hairs less private or guarded, or her hand less threatening than a strangers' – stranger than what, now? – and that at this moment it's right to focus not on the gesture but on 'the gesture,' some imaginary overlay, not really an embodiment because What's the body of 'the gesture' after all, rather the projection of one fantasy ('She wants') onto another ('Us together'). They've momentarily arrested this competition to see who can appear least competitive, whose private ruleset more straightforward, whose identity most secure. She took the day off – from whom? off what? just listen, friend – to be with him, as if bodies be rather (other) than spirits, as if the assortment in space of this submolecular permutation means 'anger' or 'gift' or –

– or 'love' –

– and yet it hasn't all fallen apart, somehow, yet. Has it? Shouldn't oughta keep score. For the moment forget how we got here, try not to worry about how *they* got here, whose bed it is (having assumed property it's almost shameful to ask you to assume propriety), where bedbugs lived before there were beds, what name they had, how they developed this fondness for mattresses and how exactly you get them *out* ('out'!) once you've got them…there are no bedbugs here, by the way. C'mon, this is a tender moment. Don't ask how I know. I was a lover before this world. Divide the time into seconds, thousandwise into milliseconds, Assume Time by the way as both medium and measurement; and just suspend one moment, (press) Pause if you can – is *that* your superpower? couldn't you have said something? – look at 'em. This array of sliding timescales, guidelines written along the cardstock gameboard's edge, not *being* but reference: stop them. Stop all of it. Rest for a measure.

Quietly now.

Her hand, there, on his cheek. A stray droplet stolen from the surrounding sea, bodysalted. Just there on his cheek. How very unlikely and yet. He opens his mouth. As if to say, one assumes, something or other, well-intentioned we hope, for her, for his lovely silly…Hold it a minute. He – he doesn't know what he feels, what feelings are, how they got here, who pulls the cord that started it spinning, how many in a mile have felt this or any one way before, what name did the city bear before names were knowable, where is the sky pinned to the earth, what's a cloud's edge exactly, what purpose does it have to name a home and for what disinterested judge and how do I find one, how do I get *back*…he chooses to live in a world named It's Funny But I Feel This strange sort of faith that she loves him. They feel wonderfully alone together, his next whispered worlds are for her only.

Leave love to lovers.

Play our passage. Looks like it's you and me now. Watch as we go: every creature in its own way and time playing the game of things, ringed all round, concentrically. Up up and away! through each magic circle in turn, up through the clear blue sea, to our (your) ocean of beckoning stars. A bit much with the talking? OK. Tell you what: let's have a game. Last one home's a rotten egg.

❤ ☞ ✤ ☞ ✳

World at night. Blue pallor steals over white objects, red and blue sink down to black. Myrmicats limp home after incursions against rival colonies' territories, black blood trailing, their exoskeletons reaching for glints of moonlight between tree branches whispering. The light is a physical thing, cool, able to slow hands and moving feet. It's a place you enter into. The cats make no sound. Dead leaves bear their weightless trundling without even a rustle. If you are very unlucky you might see them and they might see you. They eat us. They hunt us.

Mortuus est in tenebris mundi. They began to reappear one by one ten years after the last living human (a child named Tin, barely thirteen years old) set off across the Depth in a handmade boat. They were silent at first but not for lack of speech – rather their will to learn, to go about unseen and enter secret innerworlds, was greater than their need to announce their presence.

After ten years or so they began to appear in greater numbers: groups of five, ten, up to thirty or forty would rise up out of the ground together, large swathes of vegetation dying instantly wherever they passed through the ground and out into night air. They abhorred daylight.

Loose family structures sprang up, clusters of four or five helping one another to acclimate to this new world; then the beginnings of a culture. The nature of each death, much moreso than the life that preceded it, determined the character of a ghost: violent deaths tended to produce angry spirits, not surprisingly, while a long-forgotten era of prosperity had left millions of happy old people scattered between oft-visited, well-kept cemeteries – and now birthed a startlingly well-adjusted, easygoing population of 'old' ghosts.

The elder spirits taught the others to sing; and within fifteen years or so an odd tradition had sprung up, of communal Singing at sundown, and this Song was said to have been 'handed down' to the gathering remnant by one or another mystical means, presumably by the same means which led to the mass resurrection in the first place. Perhaps Tin had sung that Song herself, as she set out to die at sea.

The Song of Passing is the most beautiful sound ever to be made on this world.

Each species of animal or plant seems to respond to the Song in different ways.

Birds with white feathers will wheel erratically about a nearby cluster of dead, not as vultures would circle a carcass in wait, but like a mentally unwell person returning obsessively to an image, only occasionally flashing lucidity and seeming to reflect. Black-feathered birds are unable to fly at all while the dead Sing. Brown birds can only listen for a few moments before dying of heartbreak.

Dogs join in the Song, baying at the ghosts like wolves at the moon – but *no sound comes out.* Oddly enough the dogs don't notice, and they continue to pantomime their own Song, their throats getting more and more ragged, their eyes reddening. The smaller the dog, the lustier the howling.

Cats stand stock still when the Song begins. They seem to be paying very close, angry attention.

The Song causes small desert-dwelling mammals – voles, mice, and the like – to be seized with the desire to taste snake-meat. The snakes then feast.

Schools of saltwater fish turn feral during night Singing. Even those with no teeth at all will turn on one another, mashing into their own children's gills at frightful speeds, pinning siblings to sharp coral spines…the yellow Bay has been known to turn a horrible crimson during spawning season. Meanwhile, salmon and other freshwater fish fluoresce beautifully for the duration of the Song, at which point their energy is temporarily spent, and they must lie still upon the riverbed, vulnerable to any attack but blissfully happy.

Flowering plants, not just night-blooming but of every variety, are known to blossom spontaneously during the night's Song. Because this exposes them to the elements, however, this eruption of spectral colour prompts a mass dying-off of local flora during dry spells. The Singing dead have little enough interest in ecology, and they know not to mourn the loss of a few flowers – in the grand scheme, as they say, there is nothing to mourn at all. And the dead are uniquely well-positioned to be familiar with the grand scheme.

Pine needles grow brittle and brown, crunching underfoot. Great swarms of insects lift up from the ground and seek out stones to assail and chew through. They mingle between species, and terrible hybrid creatures sometimes emerge from unnatural couplings.

Elephants take note of the Song, but only in a disinterested way – they acknowledge the presence of their fellow dead, and continue along the century roads to their own well-deserved, much longed-for rest.

❤ ☞ ✤ ☞ ✳

Tin's story would seem to hover in the background of this story, if this is a 'story.' And maybe it does. Maybe it is.

❤ ☞ ✤ ☞ ✳

There are no Irishmen left. It feels silly saying it. Tin was the last of the humans and she left, just a few weeks prior to what would have been her thirteenth birthday (was it? did she make it that far, at least?), had anyone been around to celebrate. But birthdays had long since gone from *Fun Occasions for Parties Among Friends* to the much grimmer, much more tonally southern-gothic *Somber Occasions on Which We Make an Effort to Remember How Real Our Lives Were, in All Their Complication and Messy Humanity, Prior to the* **Horror**, *Not That They Were Good But It Was Life, Is What It Was, and We Lived It* &c., &c., &c. At what passed for Tin's ninth birthday party someone made a comment that there were no more Irishmen left, that Ireland had simply ceased to be, at the exact moment the Horror first revealed itself.

(It had gone on for some time, of course, but everyone remembered that first moment. The face. *Its face,* smiling.)

But someone mentioned Ireland being gone, just realizing at that moment that an entire nation was no more, and after a moment of recognition and startle and mourning some 20something American asked, 'Do you mean Ireland or Northern Ireland?' No one knew how to answer. (What would *you* have said? This is your world too, after all.)

The awkward silence that followed, in which no one knew quite what to say, was the closest that Tin's parents came, after the Horror, to experiencing Life Like It Was Before. The stupidity of the question, its earnestness, its absolute humanity – because after all, nationalist insanity and other forms of literary overinterpretation don't stop being important just because billions have died by fire – in that moment Tin might have perceived, however dimly, the world that the Horror had been meant to do away with.

It did not fully succeed until she gave herself to the sea on a Tuesday, quietly resolute, squinting out across the Depth at the dark spot she had convinced herself was a rescue ship, or the Three Families. She pushed the raft out until she was shoulder-deep in warm water – afraid, for just a second, to clamber aboard and separate herself finally from the earth – but a bird sang and the sun leaned around its cloud-corner, winking all asmile; and Tin pulled herself out of the water, looked back at the shore once (it was already growing small, even as she herself grew immensely large, the Last, the bravest girl on earth), and then turned toward her own death.

❤ ☞ ✾ ☞ ⁎

Chameleons' pebbled skin rapidly changes colour when the dead Sing. The Song seems to physically *touch* the lizards' skin, and splotches appear in weirding hues no living creature had ever displayed, before the Singing began.

❤ ☞ ✾ ☞ ⁎

The strangest thing about the Song, in a way, is that those who died after the Horror – whether from its touch as it scrambled up from the sea floor, or frozen by its gaze, or from fright at the possibility of experiencing that intensity of mere truth, blackly embodied – are forbidden (by unknown means) from joining in. Ten billion dead now raise bonedust voices together, but another six billion are forced to sit and listen impotently, wearing expressions of the deepest suffering.

The true Horror may well have been the sundering of the human race from its relationship to those humans who had come and gone before.

This Horror manifested in other ways.

In the last months of the human race, Tin had come under the shared protection of three families – Rose, Wolf, and Wood – who had banded together to defend a grove near the pebbled shore of the Inner Sea from marauders, and who had voted to accept Tin as one of their own when, on the brink of starvation, she came to them begging for food. Her own parents had died during the early days of the Horror, just after its dark revelation; or months had passed and they had succumbed to the unknown illness which ravaged the Americas not long after; or they had fallen when millions of coastal-dwellers were eaten alive by insects during the scouring of the human species.

She couldn't even remember.

Mr and Mrs Rose, mid–40's and childless, believed that Tin was telling the truth about this curious hole in her memory. 'She's lived through the same nightmare as the rest of us,' Mrs Rose said to the others during their fateful discussion. 'I would happily forget too, if I could.'

'Hell, I *have* forgotten most of what things were like before,' Mr Rose said.

'I know what you mean,' said Mr Wood. He and his three children huddled close to the campfire. His wife had been one of the 144,000 taken up into the sky to be food for the Horror's leather-winged progeny on the first night. Providence or (his favoured theory) dumb luck had spared him and his children. He would gladly have died in her place. Many nights he wished he had – and that the children, too, had not lived into this dissolute hell.

He hated the thought; but it returned over and over. He worried about himself.

Mrs Wolf, mother of a dead college-age son, eyed the others coolly. 'I'm not sure she's telling the truth,' she said, 'but it doesn't matter. We don't have enough supplies to take on another member in the camp, and unless we strike out for a better location…' She paused for effect; they'd had this argument many times before. 'Well, our luck's probably not going to change.'

'All the more reason to do the right thing while we can,' Mrs Rose said.

Mr Wolf snorted. 'All the more reason not to throw away what we have, you mean.' Mr Wood shot Mr Wolf a disapproving look and pulled his children closer to him.

The discussion went on in this fashion for some time: the Wolfs urged caution, or coldness; the Roses were true of heart, or suckers; Wood was sympathetic but wrapped up with his own children and willing to defer. Or he was a pansy who couldn't wait to die and be with his sainted wife, who was man enough for both of them.

Meanwhile Tin sat in the dark wood, just beyond the reach of firelight, and wondered whether she would die tonight, or next week; or had she in fact died already, and joined the swelling ranks of ghosts which she alone, among all the humans cursed to live in these final days, could see and hear. They gathered around her at night. Their voices comforted her.

Ultimately the group reached an almost-satisfactory decision: the Roses and Mr Wood agreed to share their families' supplies with Tin, and the Wolfs would help out with her care but would not be required to share material goods as such.

This arrangement lasted for months, with the Wolfs beginning to relax their injunction against Tin toward the end, Mr Wolf even going so far, once, as to give her his whole dinner when she came down with a bad chest cold and needed extra sustenance. Mrs Wolf pretended not to notice, then the next morning berated him while they gathered nuts during the cool hour after breakfast. 'Do you *want* to die like this?' she taunted him. 'Like a pair of fucking Neanderthals? Or do you want to try and make something *new?*'

'We're not just a pair anymore,' he replied, and walked away.

The night before the Three Families were to set out on their *own* rafts, their bearing set toward what appeared to be a distant beacon just across the Inner Sea, Mrs Wolf slipped a few dry brown leaves into Tin's tea.

That night she even let Tin sit on her lap while they told stories.

In the morning Tin was Dead.

♥ ☞ ❧ ☞ ✻

She woke a week later, unable anymore to speak a world of English, and with no one to speak it to, in any case.

Tin set about building her own raft. She wasn't hungry, though she didn't notice one way or the other; nor did she now need water. The thought of drinking didn't cross her mind in any case. She now worked diligently, day and night without sleeping, at the task of constructing a raft big enough for one child, not yet thirteen years old.

Day and night, now, the Dead gathered around her. She would carry something of theirs with her.

On a moonless Monday night she finished the raft and sat cross-llegged on top of it, eyes finally closing. She dreamed that all around her a swirl of grey mist was gathering, growing, deepening, until it stretched out as far as her eyes could see. Within the mist she could see pinpricks of living light darting back and forth like tiny fish. She realized that the lights were young souls just like hers.

Tin swam out into the sea of mist to join the other children. She felt deep peace. For the first time in memory, she remembered her parents' faces. They were kind and strong.

Tin dove deep, the water rippling through her like breath. A beautiful sound tickled at her ears. It was like singing, only not human singing, nor birdsong, nor whale calls. She reached a great depth where no light could reach. The sound swelled, here, into a very old Song. She understood its language.

She could hear her mother's voice. Her mother told her, 'I will always be here waiting for you.'

Tin heard her father's voice too. He said, 'Your Mom and I love you very much, Tin.'

Tin awoke in the morning to find that the voices of the Dead, which only she had ever been able to hear, had fallen silent. She could see them clearly, gathering around her in ever greater numbers. They seemed to be waiting for something.

She Sang to them.

♥ ☞ ✤ ☞ ✻

Then Tin, the bravest little girl in the world, sailed away to die alone.

Afterward the ghosts Sang to her.

STORY NO FORM / FORM NO STORY

That which speaks to us only speaks but afterward we will come to think it has intended to mean something. Only sound but we will dream it into music. There is a sharp difference between any two of our past lesser selves and the difference grows sharper or blurrier over time. There is no difference between our selves though we might like to think so. Meaning is found in expectation which is to say in the passing of our older selves. We never intended to end. Even accidents mean something.

That which sings to us only sings but afterward we will come to think it knew a secret place. Nothing in a song knows. The knowledge that communication is possible precedes the trust that communication is worthwhile but knowing is left to our past selves. Beneath the dead stone of what we believe is an innerworld stretching out in every direction as if glass made of water made of light and it consists in that which we have (as gift or preservation or gesture for all the rest of time) *forgotten*. Only song but its echoes as our voices come from below and inside. You have an empty space for echoing. You forget it was ever full. Look out our voices remind you of what we lost in death.

Those whom we love are only loved but in the fingertip touch or kiss and breath something passes from one world to the next outward as if song made of trust made of light. And here is how we preserve as gifts for the next world our present selves: we believe in love's meaning and dream it into a gift from our own past selves our own lost innerworlds. We are the gift. The dream is love and its preservation is (it was) life and the sight of its ghost passing through and beneath and forever from us is life just the same. Love dies as we have done but fingertips touch or kisses and what passes between are the ghosts of our past selves. From one world to every other.

♥ ☞ ✽ ☞ ✳

The ghosts are rarely totally silent, now; the chill of the grave settles on them like icy raiment, and whispering to one another is one of the avenues left to them, by which they can renew their sense of belonging, the impossible circumstance of continuing, despite what should have been their terminal transformation. Desperately they can *Be*.

But after their farewell Song the ghosts fell into a grave hush for fully ten years. All but a handful disappeared into the ground for most of that time. Indeed, their long silence began the night before she left; she borrowed their voices and they echoed after, faintly back.

(world-words like innermost of concentric spheres, recombinant sound by which wave of word is washed white, collapsing into thinny striking strain, which is music; they were music for her)

Then, having listened and having Sung, that first transmission (a power the dead could not have known they were entitled to share) now entered into the world, they fell contentedly silent. Those spirits who entered the world over the next several years were content to relearn the language of material things; every earthly sound that reached them brought with it a distant echo, the dead girl's final gift of farewell, her breaking pure perfect voice. They had no need to speak yet.

The Song of Passing is older than the idea of 'life'; indeed it is a form of life itself: an energetic phenomenon, we might drily say, haltingly emergent, faltering, but pure and present. As it predates life, it predates (and so doesn't know or care for) death. Its music is merely, joyfully *eventual*. The resurrected dead sharply feel loss, and understand its awful fullness, because they have *become* it; but the Song lifts them out of the fallenness which is such knowledge, for a little while.

Pass inward.

She became a bird and flew to a nearby moon, to breathe the sea mist that clung to her feathers and never die.

She drowned daintily down wondering, clutching a puppet that had washed up on the raft, and she and puppet caught a great rising bubble on its ascent, gently now, *gently*, and slipped inside to breathe the evaporate ocean and never die.

She spread dirt across the lashed trunks of the raft and in the dirt a great tree grew, which she climbed until she reached the very very Top, from which vantage she was afforded the experience of no longer wondering – she saw the whole world in its mereness, which is to say she became Goddess – and this wisdom gave her joy, which gave her strength; such strength as might stave off even the approach of Death Herself, if she chose, and she did.

She shattered like glass beneath the sign of the blue crescent and reformed as a tiny perfect crystal beneath the heavy sea, perfectly ordered, all experience stopping within her, without her; she nevermore transformed, and so could not precisely live, but would never simply die.

She erupted, a plume of sound rising up atoms thin to cloak the world in a layer of covering music, and each vestige of her could echo each other, a memento, a gift to all living things below (and to the familiar dead); echoing, ringing, she did not have to die, and so did not.

She lay down one day, a Song on her lips, and she Passed away.

CLOSING CHORD

Who are the dead? Every one of us, in a place we have not yet visited but will surely someday go. We'll meet there each of us in turn and as one: world of chance meeting and stories fulfilled. The Song continues all the while, until we consent to join in, and to become it.

And over all things the sign of the blue crescent flares, falters, flickers, is reborn; for other worlds will follow this one, they can and so they must, and *the signs are everywhere.*

Look, look darling, Cata please look before it passes: this world is just for visiting. You can stop by for a little while but you can't stay. You…

…you went…

…they've had an interesting time growing up. The eldest threw away much of what he was to have been and has become someone else entirely. A father not least. His baby is so beautiful you would cry, cry, cry to see him. A beautiful baby boy and a beautiful wife, strong and smart. You'd like her, mostly. The youngest worked so hard and he never ever forgot you, not even for a second. He was good to you in your last months but when you went he carried anger with him. They both did.

They took a long time to realize how *much* they'd lost.

But he grew up smart and strong, hard sometimes, like you were. And he'll make it now, he's found a place, a way up. To whatever it is he wants, when he knows. He's getting married. She's a hard worker like you were, but quiet at first. You were never quiet, not even when you held your tongue. Your eyes sang. Music surrounding. God you were strong.

This world can't have you anymore because you went. You had no choice, I know. But you are always nearby. You're always visiting. So many doors to sneak in through: so many Songs to steal your way inside of, and lift up like a voice. Like always.

❤ ☞ ✽ ☞ ✽

Underground there's no world you can see, anymore. You spend enough time down there it goes far, far away, even as ground to whatever figure you're making with your putterings or carryings-on or worried oval track-beating pacing waiting for the next shipment to arrive. Of? Of _____ from the same earthside dealership your parents contracted with, back in pre-Dawn days, raw uncut and recently even fair trade (yay!), complete with sterile applicators and $50 credit for free streaming mood music direct to your apartment's Ambient Sensurround whatchamacallit. Which broke for a full week last time you placed an order, maddeningly, so let's hope everything's in order with the hardware this time.

Even ambient music starts to get incredibly obtrusive down there. It only takes a couple of weeks. The *principle of outside* would act as a bulwark against that kind of madness, but you lose that too. The idea, even, of escape. No transformation of any kind possible. It turns out the human mind needs sharp contrasts to get its bearings, else it starts to invent them, to superimpose shapes and borders where not even a gradient is to be found; ergo religious war and all manner of schizophrenic such-and-such, or the need for so many different brands of soda pop. So those languorous synthesizer crescendos and ethereal/astral soundscapes start to get *oppressive* real fast, even when you're two vials deep into the _____ and inclined to be relaxed and open to things. The total lack of sensory variation in the apartment overpowers even the marquee psychological-defenses-lowering character of the _____, its main selling point earthside but honestly a little bit of a hassle there on the rock. If there weren't such pleasantly mild aural hallucinations to boot – usually a nice complement to the now hated mood music stream – there'd be no point to buying the _____ at all; except for maybe old-fashioned weird family loyalties. Your dad reached for the needle every weekend and you still look up to him, despite what the papers say. What *they* want *you* to say.

They're the ones who drove you to the _____, frankly. While we're on the subject. Incessant, intrusive, totally pitiless *questions* all the goddamn time for a man who worked every day of his life to provide for…for…and so what if he was a junkie? It's a charming thing for kids to dabble in but suddenly creepy for anyone over 40?

Hey, remember that short story you wrote as a 16-year-old, presumably inbetween late nights at the indoor track at school running so hard you couldn't even remember your name or what city you were in and it was perfect, desolate dead but perfect maybe for the same reason, where you joked about how the truest way to follow in a dead father's footsteps is to die of the same overdose as him, only as a kid, so it's extra sad and awful, and the bastards (all the bastards) are wracked with guilt?

That was a really, really uncomfortable story, but it's good that you got the sentiment out on paper back then, worked through some of your 'hey I know "suicide bad" and all but why not, y'know, *suicide?*' feelings in a benign 'literary' environment. Because if you hadn't, if you'd let even the faintest desire to off yourself linger until this very evening in the least visually interesting apartment on the deadest mining colony in the occupied galaxy, you'd have *offed* your fucking self after like three days. And ever since they legalized _____ and set up that incredible regulatory apparatus around it, a real triumph for the slowly liberalizing state (yay!), you just *know* they'd have kept the shipments coming and just transferred the monthly bill over to one of your husbands, earthside. Which seems funny, in a way, or maybe that's just the encroaching **SPACE MADNESS** talking, but you know you'd have felt guilty after a while. That's just the kind of 100% *mensch* you are.

Ya big sweetie.

Bikeback flyby world, the lights gone to lines, hyperextended ambient glow: *just like you.* Oh man you go a mile a minute, so fast you don't even need to look at anything. You can hear it go by, and that's enough. To know the world knows you're whipping through, quick as bad news.

No reason to believe you'd fall headfirst into the implied world filling out the third and fourth dimensions not (you'd've thought!) captured by that photograph, but there you have it: welcome to 1953, the night your parents conceived you, *in the back of your grandpa's Cadillac I'm totally serious*, and boy are they going to be *pissed* when they find out you're already interfering with their sex life and the condom hasn't even *broken* yet. Also: eww missionary c'mon guys show some imagination you're *having sex in a car for heaven's sake.*

SODE VI

once a pun time as a gallery fer way far way:

whilemean up inna dexter you got boyo he's tuned a self odor a blackity n they coetzee ampere palpate. he's like YOU WANNA GROW OGRE A DARK SLIDE n boyo luges is tamper n dries a cuddle palpate usin a sharpie what SIT-IN RIGHT THERE. only blackity he blacks im choosin a zone sharpie. he use a be space monk a fore he wan dark n came a cistern a ampere palpate. sousa no he can freight soup or nuts usin a sharpie too.

now boyo n blackity there chaplin n jawin wail there clashin sharpies. ampere jess laughlin pizzazz offs. boyo he's haydn neath a steal pillows. he's cochituate on is spinster layla what he re license he lover laika birther. blackity reams is mime tho n he's like DAMP I GOT A DODDER TOO N A BABY BOYO. TWINK SIZZLINGS! ONAN IF YOU AIM GONNA SWISH SIZE N COME OGRE A DARK SLIDE I MAY SWELL GO AXE HER N STEAD.

boyo he looses his mime then n he tacks is daddy n them sharpies what's flowerin n lashin. he cant eben leave is daddy would sitter summing like that. boyo wanna kiln mulder is daddy. he cusses handoffs jess like blackity diddim oiler inna episode v.

ampere he's jess laughlin. uh oh. grape bag ma steak! boyo puss donna sharpie n says AIM A SPACE MONK LIKE DADDY. IMA ONE WITH A LACTIC FORKS N YODEL TRANCE ME UP N OBIE GOT ME GONE INNA PAFF N YOU CANT EVER COSBY A MYRTLE MY DADDY NEVER NEVER NEVER NEVER NEVER.

ampere palpate neely schism self. FINE BOYO ILL JAZZ SKILL YA. n he shoops boyo riddim lightening blots. boyo callout DADDY PLEASE n daddy blackity things too is self LOVER POWER I CANT A SIDE n he sieze a hadesful luck inna amperes fates. blackity sieze evil innim.

boyo says PLEASE DADDY HALPERT.

blackity he pits up ampere palpate n throats im ogre a rollins n donna chav. theres all ways a chav inna clay mack tick seen. n ampere dries donna there but blackity vapors get sick too.

whilemean bility he's jess bout bloat up a dexter witness lazy gums n is missals. li'l time loft, boyo.

boyo tyke offs blackity's ill-met n unner neath theres jess oldman. olden teared. wanna go way n dry he's sorcery fir what he's dumb a boyo.

boyo is I LOVE YOU DADDY n daddy is I NO I NO.

o im crime jess tappin this out. o my gauche.

boyo traipse daddys bobby n fries outtie inna shuffle. bility bloats uppa dexter n fries way. boyo max it ouch too. handy n layla sieze whats opens out n space n layla is I LOVE YOU HANDY n handy is I ALL WAYS NEW n they fresh kicks like yon tea natures.

down a farce moom boyo hassa berm daddys bobby n is parrot joys a cause most n comes one width a fork. thin ever one cell breaks all cross a gallifrey. n tire firmly kin hurdle gether fir worth.

boyo lucks ogre n theres obie n yodel n blackity joys them. they habby. n layla drabs boyo black a cracklin fair n they sing Songs n a jingle a snoo felt ogre a livid n a dread.

❤ ☞ ✤ ☞ ✳

Slim to none world. Pinched faces. Furrowed brow all day long and tightness pervades all the body's cells. Or the world's: cities running right at late-for-schedule's knife edge, harried, hurrying. Cars careening down narrow side streets seeking seconds' advantage. Her absolute lack of interest in your smile upon her return, palpable. Can not unwind. Heart strains to beat. Or, 'Well if the problem is we don't have sex because we don't get along maybe we should have sex in order to get along,' a cretin's logic, questing. Pathetic. But they (haha you) do, try it, and it doesn't work just as you'd expect. Still the event (the attempt) serves as a signpost on the way out. It fits after a fashion. Later on remember the relationship entire not in terms of the daily exchange, or ongoing estrangement, but as a yearlong elaboration of that unprinciple, the shallowness of 'Let's fuck to fix us.' As if the process were a finger press or flip-a-switch to go; and not, say, love in the shared body, shared breath.

Dumbass as it comes. 'Maybe my body will tell your brain to start loving me.' 'If I won't succumb to the emotional blackmail of your tongue-lolling puppydog bullshit then maybe I'll be evolutionarily amenable to some kind of genital palliative self-administered, yay! Let's get right on that, vagina!' 'Probably just a single dose of the ol' Emily Dickinson will cure her lack of faith in my ability to really apply myself to problems that don't immediately map to pleasure! By which I mean missionary intercourse. Just a quick in-n-out, no sweat. She'll hardly know what's hit her.' 'I'll always love him and I know he loves me but my love for him is generous and his love for me is pathetic.' 'She'll always love me even though I don't deserve it because she's good not like me but the instant she lets another **pig** touch her that whore and I are through.'

Y'know: romance.

Crisscrossing what seemed to be the whole crumbled or rebirthing world, old but newly surpriseful, two three times a year looking for a principle of pursuit; I mean to say looking for whatever it is that people are known to have looked for, across years and decades from which you've come to regret your absence over the years. But a world only in the sense of, naturally, a horizon of possibility, or of knowledge; there was a Beyond, or at least a Besides, out past blackening nightborders, but it was beyond the point. Or beneath you. It's easy enough after a while simply to point the van down the fastest-moving highway lane within easy reach and make of the hour a *movement* – give yourself over often enough to that loop's languor and in time you may lose what roots you to any present spot. (A point has no substance or place: only surrounding.)

There was a rock band.

Or hothouse jazz, deep blue southern wail, spry mountainside reeling, greasy guitar documentary; or a skinny girl in leg warmers and a knit hat recollecting the musical litany she came up under, her grandmothers' musics. Or a multiply addicted Russian from Chicago who thinks so fast on his guitar you wouldn't believe it, but in two years he'll be dead or demolished so follow fast.

And there was a chance to chuck everything and empty out what you'd begun to think of (as) yourself, and you took took took it, so here you are, as American now as civil obedience and stockbrokers and freezer-packed pie, chasing the story of a true thing which once grew deep beneath the shared skin, feeding the shared body. Didn't young people choose how they might grow old, once? Wasn't there a straight safe broad sunbleached path which a thousand generations (or at least your parents' generation) beat on down for those to come, for you, thickly overgrown now? Without any responsibilities to speak of you could unmoor yourself, kick loose what timepieces had gathered parasitic upon your body. Why the fuck not. There'd be money, presumably; or, OK, hopefully. As if the difference is so simply recognized or named, for folks like you. Us. Presumed-world entire. Jesus, you've never worried a word's worth in your life. If it's life.

So then off you go. And here you hear:

Summer sheds for downwind fried-funk open-air sloven unfurling. Alpine Valley, Star Lake, Deer Creek, Shoreline, Desert Sky, the Gorge. Small stadia and amphitheatres roiling thick air through Fall Tour and into windwhipped winter, tight wound prickpointed surgical jab and sword, spiral whirl of psychedelic noise clamber up out of Rhodes piano and bounce hard off sparking bass guitar slap sawtoothed. Names that every generation learns again, then loses – names going away, becoming only *brands*. The Mothership. The Knick. The Garden. The Centrum. The Palace.

And for Christmas look forward to New Year, tripping toward the other Garden, or no now Fleet, and but now some other goddamn bank's name but the parquet still moans as ghosts pass. Damn. Folks have *died* for this place. Ringing grand circle song at midnight counts down, a great light, *auld lang syne* spoken soundwise. Cheers to Mr Burns, beastly dead, for olden quaintly beforethought endeavour a landslide (just the sound of it, *listen*), and find yourself a city, a city to live in…

(Did I forget to mention Memphis?)

World's contours traced timely, unspaced: highway distances collapse into unweighted graph's edges, the whole country's a map of our shared imagination (*but it all works out; I'm just a little freaked out*), at 3am through brokedown van windows the country's a past light – if there's a world out there anyway it wanna peek out from underneath the mapmaker's signature, our penstrokes Woven across dark fabric of Get Get Get to the Show (reverie ends, world ends, new world borne by new light), the Show, damn baby the Show…

For a couple of years in there you hardly listen to anything else. Weirdly you're not the only one. It's surprisingly easy to give over to a purely internal logic like that; so many other things work that way without troubling to be groovy giving and game. Party politics frinstance, like Aunt Sheila's, oh my god. The whole point of getting out into the world with its distant borders waving in summer heat (or blanketed in snow that frosts prickly down unto blue ice crackling clear) was to unmake the monomyth you threatened to become, right? To unhear for a while the story that falsely insists upon Oneness. Received truth. It's so lonely. To find out if the overheard mutter and wave swish whisper (the sound, the *Show*) really was the party you always thought everyone else was having, strangers you envied even in their Strangeness, abstractly. You always wondered whether it was fun they were having, that Weird wail, the enciphered language that snuck in under slammed doors against unwelcome cold (can't hurt you) or windows keeping good families safe from bad families (can't hurt you). Difference itself. Which springs from the world-that-is-the-Self too, though back then you hadn't taken enough drugs or dwelt long enough naked abed after the gold glow of blissful gethering had faded (that smile of his or hers dissolving impurely beautiful to an evening light, peaceful utterly and yes new) to know that. But Aunt Sheila, bless her heart – what a life she's had, you know? whereas Mom got all the luck – with Sheila there's a point where no amount of teenage trauma can justify that level of histrionic brittleness and passive aggression, or frankly just aggressive passivity, see she's too Correct at the level of her ideas to need merely to be Good at the level of actually just for once coming down from her soapbox-mountain fastness and y'know heading out into the word…

(there's that world again)

…so maybe what you're atoning for isn't just being born a couple decades too late to ever believe the crazy story that the world could be known, that a tank of gas and a wild spirit or whatever could ever be enough to carry you all the way past the idea of borders or mere being to to to the threshold of revelation, where you might become air, might *sublime* – but, nah, atoning also for the monomyth, or maybe we mean the *monologue,* a world maddening small speaking with one insistent voice, void, drowning anyone else who'd brave to speak. Not just Sheila, who when you've calmed down a little you can totally see why she'd defend herself, even after the murder of her guardian selves had long since come to completion: why she'd wish to be a whole person, a closed shape or line, even if she were shadow inside; nope, the world you're after is to be purposefully and purely and ecstatically incomplete, never to worry, never to part, never to take unnecessarily or sicken into selfishness – *oh* – it's the very idea of ever being *finished* or *whole* that clutches at you, black laughter nightmerrily at exposed edges of your sleep. (So long since you soundly could sleep alone; then again, neither could you dwell too long alongside anyone, inside; will we confess…?)

And yeah every Show is different, every night it's some other city's right-angled steel bone structure (clackity jack skellington makes of the lord's house a home wheresoever creep cold fingerbones catch hold, skin of earth or heart of stone, never you leave a child alone; he's an American too like you and you'll be someday a skellington too *like the rest of us*), or a campground near enough a theatre near enough a town; and they 'jam,' you're always trying to explain to your friends or whoever, twenty minutes tracing skyward a wildening helix, eight hands twined as base pairs, *perfect concord.* (God amighty you wish you could birth a noise so finely formed, is that what gifting birth feels like? Or *being born?*)

But you live in the collapsing graph edges, the higher Way,

not those disembodied points. The music falls away night upon night to become beacon – huh – or to beckon, I mean, children not yet conceived of…they'll record the notes and stops and lines but your own presence won't quite make it onto the tape. 'Remember that security guard who…I was there, y'know?': but now you're not. Rather the place you dwell, untimely, I mean timeless, is that *between* where you spent much or most of your life anyhow. We can't bear to be nowhere in particular but where else ever have we been? Your Virginia isn't mine, nor the hunter's shed lent by generous friends where your slicksweet spiriting lips first found his, nor your spot alongside the stage at Limestone that later on in summer (in summer it's always late) where for days upon hours she seemed glittered golden to dance laughing toward you, eyes, mouth, hands, her *light*…

That world America is after all only you. That body.

Your body which dreams out to us.

Our body —

now then

Time pools around us, gathers strength for further descent, the current growing stronger; and we're lifted up (oh the sky grows wider where forever she lives, but tearfully lives-no-more, gets closer and closer still) but deeper the water and darker it grows, inward its pull and the skin grows cold; time is a drowning, death is a sea, and there is the Song which buries the living. You'll unmask (loving you will unmake) the melody of me. This is the world's becoming: this is the life of our time: the war in the world it wears at our words, we weary and wild, we drown to the deeps and dream of defeat; *time is death, time is our death.*

Though stillness too is to die by degrees. Right? Well, that's the litany hushfully repeated night by night in hotel rooms or unwinterproof tents hastily erected in the clear of brownian smoke from your inherited Good Old Dad's hatchback auto, resistant in meaning to mythmaking. No one rhapsodizes about a fucking hatchback. Well but there you are, waving away the last of the Economy fuel now glassed brownly and dissipating, ears still ringing to late Show's hardsteel waveforms redoubled by concrete gymnasium walls, *remember your earplugs you idiot,* and today ya defy any mythologizing impulse **Casper the friendly zeitgeist** might have, you're in the hatchback, fuck off, and if you're committed to anything (which you are, you absolutely are) it's

1. never to lapse into stillness, which is invisibility,

2. nor to look squarely into the flaming Sauron-eye of the past,

3. nor the waiting mouth of the future,

4. and plus *the Show,* the Show, gotta get to the Show…

Not a bad agenda for staving off self-sight, all things considered. Whatever car you're driving. It was van but now, a quickling few paragraphs on, it's the hatchback. Because embarrassment too is a kind of defensive posture. You hold your own actions at arm's length, alternating goofball flop-arm flouncing about (by posture alone let the Suits know you are flatly uninterested in whatever logic of forward progress they're peddling this decade) and painstaking arcane somatic spellwork: effort in concert to conjure from thinning air a time, or perhaps a graceful state, which you were forbidden by chance or unannounced choice from achieving naturally. Born too too late.

Damn! Whose fault is it you missed the Sixties the first time around?

(Not to nitpick here and don't take offense but umm maybe if you hadn't interrupted your grandparents doing it up missionary style in the Caddy...?)

But no amount of involution or arms-crossing, no level of detailed setlist-archive collation or maintenance, no guilty canonicity of escape-dreaming (the wild world you long to visit is the *safety* of *away,* the – wait what was it – straight safe broad sunbleached path beat on down just for you and me by the very souls we now are sworn to resent and to betray and, crying ourselves to sleep night by night in – what was it, wait – inherited homes, or hatchbacks, some day invariantly to *hate,* but they made it and they fled there long before you had the wit or will to be blue), can hold back the current's rise nor the dark deep's clutch and greed. The music falls away. Cities fall away. Worlds away. Words weakly away. You. Will die. They within the music will die without it. We of words inaudibly will die.

(no Song of Passage will bear across the bonebrittling sea the nightward linger of her lips) (i'm there at limestone stamping all of us our muddy feet wailing *yes* into the bliss of dissolve and death when it comes will be only an intrusion of allwhite light into endless dark that was life of the body the body our body) (sweetsoaked do you bear upon warm skin still my love such a mark as a kiss leaves, even there, even as i)

❤ ☞ ✻ ☞ ✺

Kids' world. Sounds nice but tough going if you don't know what you're getting into. So easy to forget that you were ever guiltlessly irresponsible, or guiltlessly anything; in fact forgetting is a survival skill. You have to put all your old discarded (or vacated, or exiled) selves behind you and boldly become...less. Or so it seems on darker days. Other days it's like you just have to focus, choose to become something *in particular* rather than continuing to just eventuate through yesterday's leftovers and today's tomorrow. Which tomorrow will be only today. Boring. Boring but it pays. Boring but what pays the bills is devotion finally to the idea that, sure, you're the most important thing in the universe, but you have to go about your selfish business as if you were serving some high ideal, the Group maybe, or the Future, the very Next Generation who look up to us and for whom we can never be people (not anymore, sagging and failed and so tragically *past tense*) so we've got to resign our selves – there's that world again – to being Role Models. Ugh.

Many houses are in trees because, obviously, kids love climbing trees, and so also because that way bears won't eat you while you sleep. The bears talk, by popular demand. They say the most *outrageously* ridiculous things, baldfaced lies mostly. The popular line these days is a kind of ongoing collective improvisation with the bears about how human beings descended from honey, and how the fact that Ursa Major is the Big Dipper is some kind of cosmic signal that human beings' species destiny is to be bear food. The kids love hearing the bears spread their grotesque bullshit around the place, but the parents – whose lives on this kids' world are complicated, as you'd imagine, in so so many ways – well they worry about a race of bears capable of understanding not only constellations and their particular mythological referents, but species destiny – destiny at all – and, most worryingly, *natural selection* itself. The bears do not revere Darwin like the 101-level secularists but they do respect his insight.

Bears have no time for Freud or Marx though. *Honey bears* in particular are almost sociopathically materialist and selfish. They take no pleasure in others' lies – only their own, which they enjoy as private world-constructions rather than forms of social intercourse. As you've no doubt already figured out, honey bear literature is a load of highly mannered *bollocks*.

But they're not 'treehouses' in the classical sense, is the thing. They're actual houses, McMansions some of them even, which nestle between the broad straight strong boughs of trees so unbelievably large that they contain entire neighbourhoods. Oh, to be an 8-year-old child living a thousand feet up in a clutejohn tree and never even meet the kindhearted Tibetan family just a few hundred feet further down *toward the bears!* But of course the Tibetans have little interest in the tawdry goings-on of middle bough culture. They're way too worried about becoming breakfast for any pathologically lying man-eating bear who happens to trundle by. Also worried about China.

Adults are forbidden from working long hours, at least in theory, which affects productivity in a raft of complex ways. But what really stickies the whole situation up is that there's an office of somewhat addled, unusually officious little toddlers who have for whatever reason been put in charge of making the work schedules for each week. They're terrible at delegating. The toddlers make the schedules by finger painting all over timesheets which, even paint-free, would be textbook examples of incompetent information design and usability. Some poor schmuck at the Workfare Office – which yes, Workfare, because the kids' world tends to skew neoliberal right now; it's a time of plenty and selfishness reigns – needs to interpret the mess of paint and turn it into a schedule. His degree in Art History (not so useless after all so haha Dad) is the single luckiest selfish decision in the history of the universe.

Daddies aren't allowed to grow beards unless the ruling party specifically requests it – in which case daddies are *required* to grow beards. Fashion has not yet been invented; attention spans are too short, which is saying something. *Dungeons & Dragons* is one of more than five hundred state-mandated national pastimes, but crucially, it is only played with real dragons. [1]

Despite what one would think, the highway system in this paradisiac realm has never had a chance to fall into disrepair; the reason for this happy state of affairs is that unhappy state of affairs whereby the kids voted *unanimously* to put a tribe of friendly sugarchimps in charge of the Bureau of Gettin' Round (BGR). This wouldn't have been so bad – as of this writing, the present Secretaries of the Interior and Commerce and the head of the Dept of Transportation are actually bonobos, a race of morally enlightened Great Apes known for (1) compulsive masturbation during Cabinet meetings and (2) an uncanny knack for resolving commercial/residential/industrial zoning collisions without lasting acrimony, mainly because their working groups for handling such matters are invariably just pretty much straight-up continuous orgies, and therefore very very laid back – but the BGR is known for its unusually generous *office snack policy*, rivaling even the Department of Architecture at the *Big Boy and Big Girl 'Learning Shack'* for sheer sweet/savoury profligacy. And the one thing you can't do around a sugarchimp is provide free unlimited jellybobs and sudberry-flavoured bumbumarangs…

So the BGR is able to keep the highways well-maintained due to its policy of literally redrawing the highway system map every few months. Usually there's just enough time for about a weekend's worth of frazzled mommies and daddies shuttling their boss-children between low-gravity dance classes and non-confrontational memory-exploration therapy and Premier League Football matches (favoured to win this year, like every year: the goddamn sugarchimps, who're hard to deal with on account of

---

[1] See 'The Bit About the Dragon,' below.

the way they flounce about after even the lightest brush on a fair tackle like the Italians just begging for a gimme penalty from the referee, willing to utterly debase themselves in the name of drama and nationalism), then on Monday the roads get torn up again by a construction crew which by now has absolutely the highest ratio of *froid* to *sang* in all the dodecaverse, and it's back to the freehand drawing board for some more 'civil engineering.'

Conscientious sugarchimp objectors like Bongalow the Brave and her consort Spruce Juice are occasionally heard to complain that their species has fallen embarrassingly short of its *own* species-destiny – what a weird concept for these animal peoples to be obsessed with! – but probably this habit of nagging and harping is nothing a tasty sweet Mountain Dew wouldn't fix!

THE BIT ABOUT THE DRAGON

There's a dragon. Dozens of them, actually, but one Boss dragon named Cocoa plays a central role in this story, as in so many others. Cocoa says to the mayor of Casterbridge, 'I could use a live goat for my lunch today.'

The mayor (Ashley, age 9) says, 'I don't like goats!'

Cocoa says, 'No one does.'

Ashley says, 'I have a pebble with the Virgin Mary's face on it! My auntie Ai-ris gave it to me.'

Cocoa says, 'Who?'

'Ai-ris!'

'No, I mean who's the Virgin Mary? Or rather, given the nature of kids' world, aren't there quite a lot of those?'

'You're funny!'

Cocoa blushes, then gathers himself. He will not be put off his task today. 'Give me a goat.'

'Goats smell like a bathroom!' says the mayor.

'Yes,' says Cocoa.

'Do you want to play horsey ride?' says Ashley. Her smile is radiant. She is a career politician.

'Certainly,' says Cocoa, 'so long as we pick up that goat first. I am hungry.'

'OK. Climb on my back and we'll fly over there!' says the mayor of Casterbridge.

Cocoa does so, and they pretend-fly over to the Goat Store. The trip takes five months, because it is *miles* away and Cocoa weighs a hundred tons and Ashley is nine years old. Cocoa dies on the way. So does Ashley. The entire population of Casterbridge is shattered by this turn of events, though no one can say it's entirely unexpected – *Ashley was prone to that kind of vote-getting stunt,* the local gossips and newspaper pundits say (after a respectful silence).

The bigger deal, as far as the local nerd population is concerned, is that with Cocoa out of the picture, due to the absolutely insaaaaaane federal law about using real dragons only, getting a proper *D&D* game together is now a giant! pain! in the ass! Not least compared to, say, the equally strict laws around 'Monkey in the Middle,' which (given the explosive growth in sugarchimp population that occurs exactly nine months after the local Sugar-Mart gets restocked) don't really pose anywhere near the kind of logistical problem for hardcore gamers that the whole dragon thing does.

❤ ☞ ♣ ☞ ✻

Goblins. Goblins everywhere: in closets, hiding behind bushes in the park at night, lurking inside everybody's laptop computers waiting for just the right moment to leap out and erase some important files (like a child's most recent *Barfworld.app* savegame file, with its crucial data about the child's choice of her character's colour and style of jaunty Adventure Barf Hat). Oh, what a tangled web we weave. This is the sinister side of child-rule, or its tragic dimension: their nightmares, too, run riot, not just in terms of policymaking (the War on Really Terrible is, as so many tiresome Internetwork wags are happy to point out, nearly thirty years old at this point, with no sign of stopping) but in those dark spaces just beyond the burnt edges of the treasure map. The world has come to be defined as much by the scary things lurking about, waiting to devour it, as by its aspirations, embodied in the shining beacon of neoliberal pseudo-democracy that has its seat of power in the Big Blue and Green House at 1600 Transylvania Avenue.

♥ ☞ ♣ ☞ ✳

Inner city surface world, circulate:

Explosions over the horizon of sound. Landscape surface a drum. Buildings taking on strange waveforms: macromolecule dance. Atmosphere abruption about the pinpoint tops of great steel buildings, ball lightning following the cymbal splash of rain following the kettledrum downbeat of summer sun. Something is burning. Rain can't put it out nor put out the devotional music of feet spilling over sidewalks and flowing stepwise and hastily shoved (or affectionately steered by loving hands and arms) into the centers of streets. City blood flow like trafficking footfalls. Look here, handcart filled with frozen foods, wheeled pocket universe age-iced, giveaway tell, a halo of cold surrounds and creaking wheels foretell too. His name is A___ and he rolls the cold with him down an empty alley to make easier time at the commuter hour. *Hrm mmm hmm* humming as he comes and goes. As a younger man he saw himself as if always from a bird's vantage (the hawk's kind eye for the rabbit's devotion) revealing geometries of physical memory, slow curve across the Park, jagged sawtooth Streetswise, doubling cross diagonal an intersection with right-angled long lights, two of 'em. The point of fluxion at idle trip's midst. But A___ is old enough now to fold two prolonged adolescences into his life's span with room enough left over for a worry-free early childhood's worth. He sees the projected mood of the music he sings quietly to himself, spare syllabubs, *tum* and *de* and *ba doob* even. The buildings take on his feelings' colours as he comes and goes. Up the alley down the walk, up the way across the path and back along the thoroughfare. He's always loved the sound of that world. Hums to himself and breaks into subvocal song as he presses on. Crowd gives way like mist and then is behind him. Children's feet stamping, the wave pulse of flocking movement. Feels like he's been old longer than he was ever young. To young eyes he slogs or shambles, hauls his weary ass citywide scraping for business, a dollar-fifty for a frozen treat here, two bucks a throw gets you vacuum-packed something and the Cubans in the afternoon Tower's westering shadow love 'em (never any left by the time he comes back through Campus at evening's fall). Sure, slower now than when he and his beloved bought that second-floor apartment on Green St (older longer than ever young it now feels since she's further gone than she was ever nearly perfectly here).

But A___ has found his rhythm at least for this Day to each successive Day. It suits him fine. It suits the City fine. The sway of lofted buildings (every tower is a church to some or another busybody god he thinks) is the whole City's hat-tip honouring his labours. His bent knee groan at sunrise is a how-you-been. They are much a part of one another. Up the boulevard down the parkway, cross the northbound and hop the express, the clack racket of trackrattling trains (old worn out already when he was a young man new to this kind of being): his teeth chatter at night from cold sunk deep in his bones. He feels it the City feels it. Same bones. Same blood. Each partakes of the other's ebb flow age and cells' settling. The valve of City heart pumps once per day, the rush of lifeblood, he tumbles (rich blue red brown oxygen-filled, the currency-unit of inner aliveness), is borne through underground arteries and across sidewalk membranes bearing precious energy. She breaks you down she begs your transport she would birth fire with what you give her. (*Hrm mmm hmm.*) City's heart pulses once and relents, night comes, inward cooling rush to replenish, polyphonic burble of living river gives way to that audible exhale and diminuendo, spent, weary. Cool evening comes. He folds his proud body into a shape that no longer takes up the full space of a man. (Further gone she is than perfect nearly ever was.) Crumple of cells expiring to prepare the living ground for unforeseen living ways. They never had children, his shame. He never gave her a child. No time, not before night came, no no time...

He beats like a heart, drifts end-over-end like the great body's red cell, richly blooded, or blood itself. A____ gives no life. He and his City give and take nothing. Each constitutes each other as the body is the breath. A dollar gets you a sugar-coated, simple. The little kids by the School at midafternoon making way excitedly for home have fifty cents. Fifty cents'll do, sure. He's clear enough to see inside, window in the City wall. Misting up as if breathed upon, gently; one night he'll quiet and fold into himself and make way, within, some new kind of becoming. He's the remembering body, the language. A dollar is fine, ma'am (oh thank you). Here you go son (he loves these). He's a real beauty (just five years old this week). Remember to stay cool (I'll remember mister I promise). A beautiful boy (what do you say to the nice man). Thank you, thank you. Further she is than. And then. My love you would love it so.

SYNOPTIC WORLD

light
no borders
books evolve
no shrimp
only shrimp
sentient mopeds
loss
pinched noses
kids see weave
buildings whisper
giants
blood is blue (no blues)
earth has a mouth
hell of language pedants
we never met
glass bodies
progressive adventuring primers
frottage no biggie
they met at halloween
baby birds
no memory of pain
memory IS pain
an assortment
kids' play world

sentient appliances
roach world
fuckworld
spongeworld
giant serving dish
bus driver apocalypse
musical oscillation of your
memory is touch
a snail's pace
romance
narrative wobble
marketable
conway's garden of eden (lack of confidence)
novels are blogs
no one reads novels
abe lincoln, mechanoid
melancholy horror
cards lie
cards true
inbetween
sleepy happy children
pancake
cynthia one day late
miles never died
cars way up high
alterity gospel
online arguments
(sex with britt as a distraction)
this is bad writing
healthy chocolate
columbine follies

sasquatch
san francisco
unicorn redux
a short poem
geometric anthology
no death
heartsick innerworld we know must end
i hate kids
tupperware surround
danny and kit
bananas
no phones for pigfathers
short
rexroth
cliché
ambience
her occultation
dead air
graveyard
lukacs labs
text's innerworld
rock'n'roll
mainstream hollywood film
clown
synaesthesia
naked
we were young
menarche
her dreamworld
night forest
the Song

catalina, visiting
underground is boring
bikeback flyby
old photo
starboards, episodes iv-vi
pinched faces
following a band
kids run everything
my love you would love it so

♥ ☞ ✤ ☞ ✻

And a traipse cheerfully across a table, contented. Big big deal. All those worlds arrayed on the ground like so many marbles. Big deal. Big big big but we can rest a minute.

He's sleeping. The baby is sleeping but unsoundly, racking coughs tearing at his throat. His body is too small to sustain such tremors. Every day is new being for him, but sickness seems to be some kind of total arrest. I just want to hold him still. Or all of us, really. Just to breathe slow for once. He doesn't know that our shared destination is the world that is no world: I mean what's left of us, *dust,* will turn handsomely into fond memories belonging to other people. Watch us go, yay. There's a mouse in the apartment, or there was until recently. And lead paint on the walls which we can't treat ourselves. The state says NO NO HIRE A PROFESSIONAL.

We should leave soon. No more writing a while. Mere writing escapewise thrugh magical doors conjured up private while couchsitting at naptime, baby's, perfect my son's perfect breath is sullied by coughing wracks and ripples of hot unwelcome air. Microworld within him at war, forests burning. Castles stricken and crumbled. Someone is a bastard and my hands hunger to break a villain's bones. Or to make in the air before me some sign or sigil (remember this part?) and *bloop* there's the door and *bloop* there's a futureworld consisting of perfect memories of all that went right and a fast-forward button for what inevitably will go wrong, the terror to come, ages of terror. Weeks and months. I can't loosen the knot of my shoulders and back. I haven't been contented in a while. There's your confession. Box stacks block bookshelf access and when he climbs over piles of toys to get to them my heart stutters, shatters, there's lead paint everywhere. Poisons he can touch but can't see.

It tastes sweet, you know. They tell me the poison is sweet to taste and a baby that wants calcium – wants mother's milk and can't get it – will taste poison instead. If only some elevation, eruption into distant atmosphere, safe remove: if I could fucking fly, drive fast like a car, or be again just a kid and not have made all these mistakes which now my son has to pay for, if you could hear him coughing in his broken sleep…

This obsession with the Weave. I even remember where I first heard the term, though I can't remember if I thought it first, or if we've got yet another case of my mind stealing notions uncredited as some kind of rear-guard action against a felt sense of my own emptiness…it's from a roleplaying game. Speak no more of it. And the idea seemed so fine, so true, but the guy hadn't quite gotten it: I could feel the shape of the true thing wanting to break through its false form in someone else's writing. Thinking *Maybe maybe this is a task for me, or I'm for it…* Nice thought. Well you have to lie to yourself to get things going, for instance There's an escape. There are other worlds than this. This isn't the extent, continuous, this isn't a fragment of whole afforded us but an inadequate whole of its own; and our failing senses are trumped in the Otherlife, an other instance, by some heavenly extension of the self. We can turn into angels and cartwheel across the colourless space (we say 'black') between stars. There's something after we die and it's called JUST LIKE THIS BUT AWESOMER. My son will never stop liking me for even a second. I can think my way out of here. Poison..

I'm responsible for these other worlds (I guess I mean words) much more deeply than for my own; indeed nothing but my faults is my fault, just here. Well well I suppose that's (it's or I'm) just the story of Me, I guess. Look at this intrusion and you are so tolerant, thank you so much. Because allworlds I desperately need so as not to see, through the darkening space beyond my little imaginary typing-place, this one. This one poisoned place.

What kind of person idly flips through catalogues?

Look at the burning city world. All your fault. All your fault all your fault all your fault all my fault all my fault all my fault I made it this way all my fault I would burn it down down deepening down in circles of ash all my fault. I would burn this whole place to the ground I swear. I don't even know why. I'm to blame I'm to blame I'm to blame for I'm to I I I I I I I I made him sick *don't I*. Flames leap lapping underneath the soft skin of passing birds, COME DOWN TO US, feathers singe and catch, crackling. Here they come. The fall of starlings. Night unmade. Enough fire enough anger and it'll be daytime all the time until there's no one around to complain. Everyone gets caught in it is the thing. My fault my fault I'm to blame. Anger yourself. It is a vaccine against presence.

Thinking maybe a gospel would be enough I could save myself. Forms uniting. Holy life. If a world could just be built around one special person's life and order could flow from just how much He loved everyone, aww, fluid feelings transforming all things. If some dude could just die for us and then effuse

His good vibes all over the place, fill the world, constitute it. If that could happen then this needn't go on forever. If a messiah is possible then suffering is impossible. If God is real then death is unreal. If these books are packed up then I needn't ever read them ever. They would be some other category of thing. You can't read the bricks in the house's walls or drink the paint like water or be poisoned by a word. Well – but then. But then. On the other hand. You. But on the other hand. Well.

If I could show him all I was but unhurt, and if through him please can expiation come, or clean cooling rain –

But my beautiful boy hurts –

He shat explosively and some got on his pants so I had to put those aside, but they fit so well and we don't have too many like them, and some got on my hand, so I had to clean myself while he was on the changing table, which isn't too safe. But there's a pile of stuff on the changing table including diapers because the Diaper Genie is full, and I couldn't make room for the dirty diaper, so first he put one hand in his shit, and I was worried but I can handle that. But then he reached down with the other hand and I couldn't hold both his hands and remove the diaper and keep him from kicking all over the place. And I was worried that he'd put his hands in his mouth *which he did* or it looked like he did, he touched his face at least, and I was scared so I yelled, 'Don't please Feliks damn it!' He was kicking and putting his foot right into the enormous puddle of shit in the diaper, which had by then spread to the cloth laid out beneath the diaper, but when I yelled he widened his eyes and went very still. He started to cry and scream.

He was so scared. I scared my son so badly.

So then I picked him up and ran to the bathroom, thinking to run bathwater over him, but I couldn't get the water temperature right, so first it was too warm then it was too cold, then almost right, and the water was puddling under him and turning that sickly yellow-green shit colour. I had to hold him temporarily under one arm and against my stomach so I could adjust the temperature and roll up one pant leg, and of course his shit was all over my shirt, but I couldn't take it off yet. But then all I could think was *he shouldn't be sitting on the bare bathtub surface* because I'm such a terrible father and housemate that I'm certain the tub is covered with a thick layer of bacteria, mold, mildew, viruses, tiny creatures waiting to infect and harm my son, even though every night I dump out the humidifier and the tub ends up full of bleach, but you can't see anything, how can you know? But I sat him in the water and was able to turn him around to run the bathwater over his ass, there was shit coming off him in thick rivulets and running over to my foot, streaks all along the tub. I had to set him down on the bare surface to wash his hands, and while scooting him around in the tub I bumped his head against the faucet, and *he had been whimpering in fear this whole time* and now he began screaming even though it couldn't have hurt, really, but I can't tell because I don't know anything about my son.

Then I swished him around in the yellow-green water and with my bare hand was wiping this caked-on shit layer from his ass, his feet, his thighs, but I of course have no soap to hand, and don't even have a towel, plus there's certainly baby shit on my foot, and he's *still crying because I scared and hurt him*. But I kill the water and pick him up, now balancing him against the side of my shirt that doesn't have a giant shit smear on it.

Plus I'm thinking about how the humidifier stopped working sometime last night so we're going to have to exchange it, and he and I have this identical rustling cough today, which is probably from the dryness of the air which is my fault, the humidifier is one of my few day-to-day responsibilities for Christ's sake, his sickness is my fault if he's sick, but what if it's just that he's still teething? And if the humidifier doesn't work then when will I get secondhand bleach in the bathtub and how can I keep my son from getting sick when I can't even keep his hands out of his mouth while changing his diapers? But I walk back to the bedroom with my soaking-wet baby in my arms and set him down on the changing table and have to stand there moving this pile of shit-stained clothes around on the changing pad and putting things onto the clothes pile on the floor, and now I'm struggling not to cry because I'm so afraid that he's going to hate me for the rest of his life for making him afraid of water or raised voices or dry air or the sun or just new things. I don't cry because I get angry at myself instead. The dead humidifier is there on the ground and I have to move it out of the way to shuffle all these dirty dusty useless stupid things around to make room for my soaking-wet baby son so I can strap him down to keep him from falling onto the floor while I grab a fistful of wet wipes and start cleaning his feet, hands, thighs, and especially those spaces inbetween his pelvis and thighs where everything that can accumulate between fat folds most certainly does.

Naturally he reaches for his crotch again which is what got us into this mess in the first place. I say to him as calmly as I can, 'Feliks, please STOP. Please just wait a minute,' which he doesn't understand as words but he sits still looking at me long enough for me to wipe him up, and I get a new shirt and new pants that don't fit quite as well, the tighter-waisted blue ones with the shorter legs, and I put him in the crib to change him. But despite how much he hates and fears me now and what a terrible clumsy selfish monster I am – hey what do you know

I started to cry while writing this – even as I put him down he starts crying again because he wants to be taken care of. He wants me to take care of him. I get the shirt on him, then the pants, and he plays with his zippered sleep coverall/sack while I pick a new shirt for myself, gather up all the dirty diapers, put things into a plastic bag, collapse down into myself again, reach for my baby son who is now smiling, who won't know whether he remembers this event, though I tell myself that I will, that I'll be so nice and so calm and quiet and I'll always try to keep things in perspective – but even as I say it I realize that I'll lose this memory too, along with almost every single other one, and what's left will be colour and sense: I can never do enough for this person who needs me so badly but nothing else in the world is so important to me, I promise my love, Feliks I promise you –

– but if I could be a past without pain, a world my own, finally, and no longer to block allworlds' light –

Laura the bookshop keeper is seated on the high riser in the back of the old school's gymnasium between her friends Jo and Nicole, blonde brown blonde hair in a close huddle, cheeks red smiles beaming and eyes clear. The morning passed in relative peace and ease and they feel the Festival has started extremely well this year; in high school they shared boyfriends, which everyone knows and still finds funny, and Nicole and Laura kissed in the woods after prom and all summer long, which no one knows or will ever *ever* find out. On the riser below them are Eszter and Gregor, nearly 80 years apiece, likely only staying for this afternoon's festivities then retiring early to the house on Jefferson St where they've lived all their adult lives. Her hand rests on his, weighs almost nothing; they've had a good life together and the Festival, every two years, is like a vacation. In 20 years they haven't been on a trip together, since Gregor developed his bad knee, and even then his business travel had accounted for the largest part of their journeys beyond the village limits. A year from now Eszter's other kidney will fail and she'll slip away from him, in her sleep – a year after that, he'll follow. Their breaths are steady and calm, heads inclining toward one another, and her hand weighs nothing at all. There's Karl, Laura's fiancé, hanging back by the emergency exit, smoking a cigarette; and there are Mr and Mrs McAllister, whose son died last summer while camping with friends – they need this almost more than anyone; and Dick Waters, the schoolteacher, his hearing aid no doubt lost again; and look it's old Dutch, the merry Englishman who moved to town with his wife and children a few years ago – he's dressed up as ever, tailored suit still in fine condition after 20 years in his closet ('for safekeeping – it's too good to wear just anywhere, you can wear a *rubbish* suit to church of course, but come here Wall, feel the *quality* of this'), making jokes that were old before the kids in his small audience were born. Masterful. Even his laughter has an accent – and his accent gets mysteriously thicker when he's talking to American women, of course. There's the Mayor, Mary Waters, the teacher's eldest daughter, who caused a scandal when she didn't take her husband's name and caused another by being quite a competent though obviously frustrated Mayor on the whole. She wears a blue pantsuit after a certain fashion, her hair short and streaked with red-blonde highlights (after another), and the start of the Festival of Permutation is the day she looks forward to most – never moreso than since she took over the Mayoral post, with its litany of zoning discussions and unanimous procedural votes and favours granted not to friends but to their Families' Good Names. Her husband Isaac clings to a graduate degree as one sign of his worth, and Mary as another; they met at school, and she stayed in their college town for him so long as he promised to move back with her to take care of her mother in Mom's last year. Like anything else: the last year lasted five, and they're permanent residents now, though mercifully not living with father-in-law Dick anymore, with that fucking hearing aid he's always losing and his constant comments about gays or Arabs or whoever it is he's 'just joking around' about today. Isaac is permitted to sit at the front of the gym with her but chooses instead to stay on the bleachers with everyone else, chatting idly with Laura's younger sister Lynn, back home from senior year this week, Isaac sitting maybe a little too close to her, meeting his wife's eyes maybe once or twice too often, too quickly. The smallest of things. When Mr Waters dies Isaac will cause a little scandal all his own by leaving Mary and moving back to the city; she'll take only the smallest hint of satisfaction in knowing that, in his life, he'll never be happier than when they first met and fell in love, over the heaviest gnocchi either of them had ever eaten or even *heard* of, Jesus! with that olive oil drizzled on top and the *capers*, do you remember? Of course I do, honey, how could I forget?

♥ ☞ ♣ ☞ ✳

and the thought that I
might have done something right
is a new wound

♥ ☞ ♣ ☞ ✳

Wakeup world. Slow break musical of valley dawn, sunspatters at mountainsides. Or diamond prickling distant peaks. Tip cap top all snowy. It's OK. Welcoming each of the billion into wakety wake how are you. Not in English of course but. Tip of cap all feathered. Hi Frank. Brim touched a greeting. Danny. You been all right. I been fine Frank how you been. Danny I tell you I been just fine. Lookin at that painting you gave me. Glad you like it Frank. Naw Danny I love it. That painting gives me a good feeling I can't even tell you. Pleasure of confession (the truth ought out) to kick off the day beneath the honeysweet splash of new light amountainside. Down here the village gets up at morning to say, altogether now, How ya been.

Mrs Hertzl. How's your mama been Ace. Aww she's great Mrs Hertzl. She's doin great since the storm stopped. Ace you wouldn't know this but ever since we was girls your mama had a queer thing with those storms. Yeah? She used to get so caught up when those storms'd come. Yeah? Yes indeed, I remember one time when we was goin on eight nine years old there's this dreadful rattle up the bell tower at the Hall, but the wind hadn't even started yet. We could see them lights off east of here up by Ed Watson's place. But no wind yet. Strangest thing. No way, that's pretty weird! Indeed…but your mother – funniest thing, your mother she was out there in your grandpa's field, out where he grows alfalfa now but back then it were totally empty actually. We all went lookin for her to make sure she heard that bell tower rattlin but when we found her she was out there in that field. Can't remember why, now.

Yeah? Mrs Hertzl what happened then?

Well she's in a strange way, Ace. She's in a strange way that day. I'm not sure I even remember to tell you the truth.

Awwww!

No, I think I won't remember that today. You go on now. You tell your mama all that's left of us we know she'll be OK. Take care now Ace.

Where things happen small and large and the space contracts

or shuddering expands to fit the work within. Wordbuilding.

Funny thing, we found her dancin out there in your gramp's empty field. She was dancin and the wind was upon her but there weren't no wind yet. Her skirts was picked up by wind almost over her head and she was dancin and dancin. And those bells was getting louder all the while. We never did find out what rung them bells.

Nice idea as if the morning could forget away all the night-time things creeping around at memory corners. Not all dark things are nocturnal. Anxiety is what stays – why's it here in the light when I thought I left it in the dark, why can't things be *new* just once – and day does nothing to make hard things easier. 'It'll look less scary in the morning.' But it's the eyes change, not the light; and it's us that make monsters out of neighbours. Frank borrowed Danny's hammer and never returned it, but Danny didn't notice as he had two (as it happened). Or Frank stole twenty bucks off Danny's mantel one Sunday evening after the game to pay for gas. Nothing big. It stays with you though. Danny never could look Frank in the eye after that. Not as if Danny'd done anything wrong, he just didn't want to make a thing of it, to clash openly with an old friend, especially after Frank had stayed up with Danny while his wife was so sick. It became too much: the guilt of knowing. And to have to think less of a friend. He figured it was easier to pretend he didn't know anything at all, to go on. Just one of those things Frank did over the years. You can forgive. Not the same as forgetting though. What you fail to destroy will come back stronger and pitiless. No moment comes twice.

The town's going on 200 years old, no one remembers how old exactly but the ladies at the Altar and Rosary Society, who love that kind of thing. But to talk to them about anything,

God, even a priest would pull a sour face. Mrs Coolidge on her fourth husband (and the only thing keeping him alive is Who even knows where the money is?) and you have to figure there's something between her and Father Michael. But that face. Peel paint off a Chevy in the dark. How a woman goes through four husbands without smiling, who knows.

The Altar and Rosary Society has a curious history, actually. While we're on the subject. It wasn't founded here – that is, it's not specific to Mother of Sorrows Church, the first members came from over in Lewiston, over at Blessed Name, something like 1906. And they just told the priest (Father Mike too, as it happens, though you gotta figure not the *same* Father Mike, right?) they'd be setting up shop at the church and he should set aside some time for them to say their rosaries a half-hour before Mass or what have you. That awful droning sound that doesn't really quite sound like voices. The altar boys are always too weirded out by that sound to spend any time in the church itself prior to the Mass. In fact Pete, Mrs Hertzl's boy, he actually puts tissues in his ears when he lays out the chalice and ciborium a few minutes before kickoff. The head of the Society is Mrs Coolidge – the altar boys have called her Mrs Grinch going back to basically the publication of *How the Grinch Stole Christmas*, which you have to applaud their characterological insight there – and she has a way of catching the altar boys' eyes even without looking up. It's as weird as it sounds. Like her head will be bowed in the front row (Grinch always sits in the front row like she can't even enjoy Mass unless Father Mike and the two altar boys have to spend the whole time looking at her horrible prune face) and she'll be mumbling her way through the rosary, which no matter what she's praying she always sounds like she's making a fucking *accusation*, but you head over to set out the water and wine (Mike likes a decent amount of wine, less than Monsignior drunkass redfaced saying-the-Mass-in-English-is-an-abomination and singing-at-Mass-is-for-Protestant-degenerates McCarthy but still a lot, like an amount of wine only McCarthy in this whole word would think was an inadequate amount, so don't skimp) (goddamn remember that time you were serving during a funeral and he actually complained *during the Mass* that you were skimping on the wine, like he literally yelled out MORE WINE! and you could hear this entire church full of people whose dad or brother or boss or fishing buddy just died, they all just suddenly went *totally still*?) and there'll be this hitch in Grinch's voice like she just licked her lips, you'll look over and her head will still be down, but then you'll see that fucking *face* but what's weird is it's like she doesn't move. Her face is just hidden and then it's there. Like she's always looking down at the pew and around for, like, her *food*.

Coolidge is actually older than the Society itself. No, not just the local chapter, which would still place her somewhere around 120 years old, which is just barely on the terrifying-but-fitting-in-a-mean-way side of possibility; she's older than the Lewiston chapter too. And *they* claim they were founded in 1741. Which isn't even possible – there weren't Altar and Rosary Societies back then at all! Though there was probably always some old woman ready to keep Father Mike or whoever warm when the Devil (or whoever it is who's in charge of weather) brought winter around.

Coolidge is more than 600 years old. Is there a chance she could be Joan of Arc? How did she learn to speak modern English, then? Well she'd have had lots of practice I suppose. And if she's actually Joan of Arc then that would explain the sour attitude.

And she really can look at the ground and all around all at once. Which is interesting but not all that rare. Many a mom has picked up a benign form of that skill over the many years. You've got no choice. But Coolidge never had kids. She *hates* kids. The scary thing, the scariest thing of all without question, the very thing that makes *this* town a little different from the other towns down in the Valley (what a lovely sunrise we had today, what a refreshing breeze, what songs on maidens' lips; what a day in the Valley!), is *who taught the horrible Coolidge woman the sight without seeing.*

Aah, but she's all right. Hell, she used to be a fine dancer back in the day. Not that you'd know it to look at her now – she can shrivel a testicle at fifty paces, ask her husband, ask pretty much *anyone's* husband – but back in the 17th century she loved dancing more than anything. They say she didn't even need music to kick up her feet; the lady could make a mountain wind rise up by humming a tune to herself, and the wind would whistle along, the selfsame tune. They say she's died before by fire and by cold, but won't go again until she's finished her work. Got a voice like a child trying to breathe mud.

♥ ☞ ♣ ☞ ✵

The world's dominant local predators, called 'cars' or 'automobiles' (self-movers), have overseen the construction and layout of the city such that only they are allowed to travel on the wide paved boulevards – which extend for millions of miles across the length and breadth of the country. Humans and other animals are expected to use the supplementary side-walking paths, which are only available in the dense cell blocks known as cities (and are strictly forbidden in the car-only regions of the continent symbolically known as 'highways'). Humans spend most of their time hiding from the local top predators inside their sturdy exoskeletons (equally literally-named 'buildings'). Many humans enter into symbiotic relationships with automobiles, watering them and providing fluids to drink; however the automobiles have a strong taste for living flesh (generally leaving carcasses beside the roadways). What humans get out of this exchange is minimal: the cars afford transport to linked or distant human colonies, where their human symbionts emerge from the autos' gullets and hide inside other, biologically-compatible exoskeletons. Cars apparently treat human-acquisition as a form of status improvement; cars with no human symbionts are regarded as fallen, and the lack of affective connection generally leads to decay and expiration.

Automobile graveyards are among the most desolate places on earth; not surprisingly, some humans have established religious protocols whereby they resuscitate deceased automobiles and cohabitate with their zombified corpses. Because humans are able to bend such organisms more readily to their limited wills, these exhausted 'used cars' are far more agreeable creatures than dominant automobile predators.

Unfulfilled desires make the world but they unmake it as well. Could be that's all consciousness is; and it could be (don't quote me) that consciousness is all the world is. Not to say 'the world is conscious' but that is must be conceived of, it is a dream, a unity, and all unities are imposed…that would seem only to be mathematics. Nothing more or less cynical or optimistic. What's left when the Self has settled, when minds rest: the interstice, the medium of touch. We are living in a material word. Brought into being for the purposes of connection; and there's no place that minds 'live,' no Situation; just a sense of connection.

More likely there's just one mind, though. Multiple 'personalities' if you like: Me'shell at the local beauty shop, Glamorama, who misses her baby brother; the Horsehead Nebula in its slow transit across the idea of sky; Rolling Terrace Boulevard percussive under kiddo feet's summer scamper; the next world in this commuted sentence. (It would have been: Love.) But only one mind; and so an infinite universe makes sense. Every desire would necessarily go unfulfilled and you'd need to keep on making more. Pointless really. Infinity'd be unnecessary, or at least grotesque or dumb, if there were actually trillions of folks around. Seven people could surely settle on the right amount of deserted island, could imagine Enough. Seven billion a harder time but they'd manage, or let's hope for our own sake!

But just one?

Who in that horrible instance would shame you into saying *Enough?* How would you know you had ceased to need and given in to want? Your suffering would be infinite. (Not that it isn't now, *Oh I'm sure.* But.) Indeed the universe would itself be a manifestation of your suffering. If you could conceive of every possible thing, if newborn logics of cognitive misfire could give birth to new worlds, unmet demands involuting to meet themselves, even becoming sentient(!), if the very fabric of the universe were only a half-assed answer to the question *Why am I all alone* – not even an answer-in-fact but deferral, or refusal; if you never even learned to *wait* because there was no other soul to mark the time with – why, every being, every emergent order, living or nonliving, would carry within it some miniature of the moment of creation itself, a spark, at every organizational level the cascade of *entropy* (which is Time, which is energy's own Need – for resolution, maybe); that would be desire, which would be suffering, the genetic code of all matter-energy-notion, the premise of allbeing. It'd be your fault, mind you, but on the other 'hand' you alone would bear the responsibility of blaming yourself, which you could as easily dodge – not a bad idea really! – and every being Thing would with its mere existence sing your praises, would conceive of its Self first of all in relation to you, *indebted* since creation, and that debt would be the fabric of all things too, in a way; and after a while they'd come to think they'd thought *you* into being. Every rock and fractal crenellation, every Baskerville hound and uranium atom (replaying in miniature with its slow decay the creative exhalation, the First Ever Giving-Up, your own name), Me'shell down the street and the street's own tattooed stone skin…they'd come to reimagine you, you, you at the center of all things, and then one day, Risen Up, would through their own contortions (selfish thinking along the lines of must-we-eternally-suffer) come to understanding, a new picture of all things, a language of being-suffering which would allow them to rest in their separateness, to shoulder the infinity of blame which was the first Lego-block interlock that shaped your made-up universe: they figure *they made you up*. The gall of these people…

But who are you to argue?

And so the one really noble thing left for you to do is to become the universe in its unwinding, join the entropic flow at last, become Time; and stop trying to hide your Self from yourself. See what happens when you stop abusing yourself and let all being merely be. You imagined all things into thingness, *bravo,* but now it's time you became just a thing too. Finally to exist in the language in which your creations exist. To enter into the word, which in the beginning was your message to yourself: *nice try not good enough.* How's that for justice.

So the kicker is that they never had a good reason to *love* you and were wrong to *doubt* you (admittedly that's all on them; but if you thought them into being and proper credit is a whole big thing with you, then why didn't you say something earlier?), and they're gonna be wrongest of all during the Rapture to come – your embodiment, Word made Flesh! Holy moley, the Creator joins the Creation and your fantasies will have long since convinced themselves that a Creator is totally impossible, because everything in the word is *fantasy;* holy holy moley. Are you eve gonna come as a *surprise.*

Talk about shooting yourself in the foot, publicity-wise! If you had a foot.

So drop on by if you want, peacocking a little if you like as you are, after all (by a factor of, um, not a number but indeed of Quality), the single most accomplished being in the spaceless placeless universe – though admittedly you started with some advantages and set the game's rules yourself; if any being or concept ever to exist is 'the 1%' then you most definitely are the youdamned 1% – but prepare yourself for the mild blow to your self-esteem that will come when no one is really convinced that you are who you say you are. Maybe set some plants on fire, tend some sheep, get nailed to a tree. Or you could be a whole planet if you liked. Join the Catalogue: leaf through and insert yourself in the form of a new Word. Move over the surface of the waters. Join the Song. The best feeling will be to merely be. You can permit yourself to exist, but that's it: that's the end of your privilege. Once you begin to live you'll care no more for Control; *life is its opposite.* Even in its wild complexity of self-organization, its hysterical clawing toward Order, life always ends up (I mean washes out – or rolls on) as flow. Which is Time. Which is Need.

And you who made the universe to alleviate your suffering,

your boundless Want-become-autonomous; you who set out to do a little wordbuilding because you felt lonely and didn't have a fixed plan in mind (is why there's just Worlds instead of Story); you, GOD, DAMN YOU: finally you can know within new bones that the Song needs resolution, that being wishes to end. You can really *really* Need for the very first time. The thing that separated you from your Creation, power which bound you up, was stasis all along. As your unfulfilled desire was the root of your suffering, your simple need (bravely experienced, truly acknowledged) will be the engine of your salvation.

And then you can finally, really *get on with it* and die. Oh, thank the…well, I suppose thank *you*.

All things will die with you, probably; they were only ever your self-conception. Your universe, your ego-defense (does God have an ego? is the idea so stupid as to shame God into nevermindness, joke Him into nothing? could be, could be), it goes when you go. Fine. You hadn't thought of that, but then *that's suffering*. What else did you (fail to) think suffering was.

Oh (allbeing is the fatal arrowpoint of Time and it pierces us, our heart, it binds us, being is dying) but it burns brightly it births universes each being unto itself it flows together (you deserved this) and living Times nestle within outer Time and that is called Place (you can feel its pull) (love is named gravity) and it

♥ ☞ ♣ ☞ ✳

Tactical combat world. Steer clear or oil up yer blackjack.

Collected worlds (complete with scholarly annotations) of authors famed for what a dude called 'subcreation': chief among them Dandrel's horrible but influential *Helion* trilogy (*Apogee, Perigee, Anapsis*). God I spent so many hours wishing I could live there. The interstellar-travel-by-giant-solar-trampoline conceit was more or less the cognitive soundtrack to my ages 13–15. Play and dissipation. So much wanting to believe that swashes would in the spacegoing future still be buckled, planks (airlocks, probably) nervously walked (or the equivalent) by those richly deserving of such mistreatment – or heroes sure (*c'mon c'mon!*) to make it Outta This Scrape in one piece. Back then there was this growing idea that outer space was at once a solved problem – ready to fade from dream to waking like a Christmas present turned out to be socks – and an increasingly distant/inaccessible bureaucratic zone, cowboys being replaced by factory farms, except the cowboys were never actually real, not in my lifetime anyhow. Machines all the way down. Nah. That tentative/reckless phase of early space exploration was done by the time I popped out. Or in, I guess.

So in order to get at the shared pre-actual-mere-*space* awe and aspiration of limitless idea-of-space, indeed the recognition or belief that a place could still somewhere exist which was *limitlessness itself*, a whole just really creepy principle, well ironically enough you had to turn back the clock a little. Big-time thing with kids all throughout history, probably: realizing first that time passes, then finding a way to escape into a new present which was the past's future, today what shouldabeen. You dreamed of being an astronaut, but always as somebody's angry libertarian writer grandpa had imagined it: the spacesuits less marshmallow, more race car; rocket ships like big sleek motorcycles, or just nuclear-powered flying cocks pretty much (because of course *that* – the implied parallel term, ahem – was the other forbidding limitless void to focus on, back then, after you'd learned that babies come from there but before you really internalized that *holy shit babies really actually come from there*; and maybe that's the moment Cthulhu awakens?); laser guns actual guns, instead of…

Come to think of it, that was the worst part. The further along time went, the harder it was to convince ourselves that we'd be able to defend against whatever Inevitable Menace might rear up out of the frigid wastes to, not *eat* us probably, but *digest*, or cognitively-scramble, madden, suffocate, poison, freeze, unmake us…the way grief manifested in those days was I was never going to get a laser gun because by that point it'd be utterly pointless. You didn't need one to deal with your fellow man, and even low-slung hip-holstered laser pistols (such as F.R. Dandrel's interplanetary gunslinger Tubby Crozan might wear) would be no match for bacteria that turned flesh to slime, poison seeped into the walls to turn your inner places liquid, movies so entertaining that to look at them was to will yourself suddenly toward death by consumption (by consuming – just looking into the staticky whatever it was supposed to be, forever). Fuck grownup literature. And fuck the Department of the Galactic Interior or whatever for spending all its astronaut time making microscopic adjustments to the lenses of telescopes, as if *slightly clearer pictures of nebulae* were some kind of substitute for the immensity, impersonality, the *divinity* of the frontier. It was UN-AMERICAN.

Tubby Crozan comes in for it hard in the footnotes, is one of the additional childhood-beshittenings awaiting the grownup SF fan here. The greatest of all mechanical-engineers–9th-class-turned-pistol-packing-mercenaries, the first man to make a solar trampoline jump in just a suit (not even a ship! the unmitigated gall, the titanic fucking *balls* on that guy!)…and all editor Avram U.N. Robear wants to talk about is 'Crozan, a too-obvious Heinlein manqué, comes close at times but never quite breaks with the dreary juvenile misogyny of his author, not to mention his thinly-veiled SFnal homage-referent Gully Foyle; the lasting popularity of the *Helion* cycle is testament to the guilelessness and vivacity of Dandrel's prose and his just-left-of-the-familiar plotting, rather than any psychological insight. Like C.S. Leavis's *Hornea* books, Dandrel's novels grow more difficult to like as their readers grow older; though perhaps – like reactionary family members' dinnertime political outbursts collapsing over years from unwelcome idea into familiar, almost comforting gesture, thereby losing their power to wound – for the very same reason, they grow easier to *love*.'

Robear won an award for the annotated edition, not a big deal award but enough to feel good about being, at death's door, a SF scholar of all things; and it's hard to separate gratitude for his hard, revelatory biographical work (Dandrel collected butterflies but refused to kill them, adding them to his library only after they'd died natural deaths in captivity?!) from frustration at the characteristically British is-it-really-still-*ironic*-after-all-these-centuries snippy melancholy which pervades his scholarly work. Robear (an obvious Franklin C. Kitzis manqué if you must know) deserves his reputation, though perhaps we can with a wink-n-nudge admit to one another, right here and now, that that's not meant *solely* as a compliment. Fa!

...

Damn, that felt good. I can't *tell you* how much I hate Frank Kitzis. And no, it's not because he dated one of my grad school professors for a while and was cheating on her either before, during, or after the *worst of all time guest lecture* he gave in our SF-and-feminism class, which I think he actually had the stones to call 'Criminal, Liminal, Subliminal: something something something Rosetti something something rape.' I liked that class well enough for most of its run, but maybe it's testament to every thinking human being's overall feelings about grad school in the humanities – so long jerks, by the way – that that really is all I can remember of the talk's title. And nothing whatsoever of the content. Kitzis had fashion hair, you know? The kind you're supposed to look at and maybe notice without recognizing outwardly that you're noticing it, like Wow that guy's got Cool hair, it's just so *messy*, but then it's only hours later you're supposed to realize that he must've spent ten minutes and five dollars in *product* (people just call it 'product' now) to get his hair into that 'artful' dishevelment, and the labour itself is supposed to be a mark of really caring about presentation or whatever, only *my* curse – talk about First World Problems so to speak! – is that I always notice the time/'product' costs of hairstyles right in the moment. Right there in that instant. Or like how someone's courier bag is brand new but he's walking around like he's King Hardcore Biker of Bikerville, complete with the clip-in shoes and everything, but also brand-new sunglasses that he takes off super carefully because while he wants you to think he doesn't care about the money, He cares. About. The Money. Wouldn't you? That's why they call it *money*.

Or how all the pronouns are 'he' and all the metaphors are balls this and stones that, and there's some racism maybe, plus weird nationalism? And who actually thinks it's awesome that spaceships look like dicks? I notice that stuff too. But since they severed my *corpus callosum* in the course of an otherwise routine cranial probe, prefatory to my first Saturn trip (boooooooring!), even when I see my worst impulses as if secondhand, even in moments of what pre-AI cultures called 'self-awareness,' I'm powerless to do anything to stop myself.

And you know what?

'I'm a man,' Crozan said, and aimed the laser blaster at Freia's heart. 'You're a monster,' she replied. Her eyes were defiant but she shrank back. Crozan laughed then. 'A distinction without a difference, Your Highness.' He pulled the trigger, and as warm blood splashed his handsome face – her blood, his lover's blood, *royal blood* – he found that he could not stop laughing. He laughed and laughed, and in his triumph he grew larger, and darker, and more joyful…

I'm a ~~monster~~ man.

♥ ☞ ✿ ☞ ✳

Closer closer for the world is small. Not growing nor indeed alive. It has reached its limit. Run out of words it has, of world, whoops. Big things get small. I was dejected after an early breakfast and then a building fell down. Or someone knocked it down. We are the thing the world has run out of. A dog was barking and I couldn't sleep. Then I mislaid a book. I got engaged and he turned out to be someone else. My face was handsome but now I'm dead, or 33. Jesus wasn't real but now he's real – I mean He's. He was a guy and they turned him into a protagonist. They did the same for me! Thank you: or wait, I dropped a box on my toe and on Thursday there was a war in which hundreds of thousands died. The box wasn't even that heavy but it contained pictures of my mother who died, died, and I do get emotional about mistreating symbols of her. I mean of Her. Two animals ran through a field and then one animal ran through a field. The roots of a thirsting plant could not reach deep enough into the soil and the entire field dried, died; then you 'showed [someone else's child] the back of [your] hand,' in the sense of *hit [someone else's child] in the face*, and who trusts you now? But then, who even trusted you before.

The smallness of it is OK. The bigness is OK. Closer listen for the news is bad; I mean 'news' is bad: it's not new. What's coming is the same what's come, probably. Tuesday a building was knocked over, I mean everyone in it died, and Wednesday night we went dancing and they played 'Common People.' Not even space between staggers or shouts to catch breath and, what, 'live?' Oh is *that* the thing we're forgetting to do. Is *that* the... Then on Friday I transformed from a caterpillar into a bird's lunchtime meal, though then what's lunchtime to a bird? Or to me, the lunch? Birds don't have deathbeds is why they don't have regrets! Is maybe the point: the day they die is a day. It's not as if you dying was the most important thing that happened that day. Probably the message-passing mechanism within the network is broken, or conceived of all wrong. Because shouldn't a child's dying be the end of everything? Like it feels? And it isn't. Shouldn't a bird mark its last flight? Why don't they care that they live upon wind? Or on Tuesday I drank water carried from a thousand miles away, and you reached across the table touching my hand saying *God they didn't even call you back? That's such...* and the water tasted probably about the same as the tap, but I was too stuffed up to notice really. Then in December a couple of buildings fell down, or someone flew planes into them, oh what sport. Afterward an enormous brown bear reached into the stream for what turned out not even to be a fish, and its stomach gurgled and it would die soon probably. Or it slept fat and woke thin but didn't mind. Then at the summer solstice party Pete from Seattle handed out little blue caplets and everyone took them at the same time, some people prayed first even, and for a while the colours were really real, the thingness of things unimpeded by wanting otherwise; and her name was Kelly or Frida or she went by Issy or her online username and she drew comics or she was a smoker and her prom dress wasn't slinky like everyone else's or oh my god my god what was her name, we liked each other and that was enough, and mid-August everyone in one or four buildings was terrified and most of them died (crash, fire, fall, crush, starved, Terror even) or it was February and only a birthday party where only ice cream was served after the dog ate the cake. Laughing, laughing, because look at the dog! She's sick, stupid dog I love you! The world it's small, closer closer because to keep each other *warm*. That should be enough, it won't be enough. There's no such thing as enough anyway.

Did you ever notice how all your ex-boyfriends are totally different human beings? *That* world, radiating in *that* sense, *that* growing sphere, the mathematical idea of it: I promise that that that that *that* will never run out. Getting bigger all the time because you no longer demand to be able to hold it.

I wish I were a totally different human being. And then

❤ ☞ ♣ ☞ ✳

poof well whaddaya know

❤ ☞ ♣ ☞ ✳

In the whole world only three children's librarians, haircut each carefully to comfort (the afflicted), dressed each for work daily in floral prints under knit sweaters in bright colours, each able to conjure even at 4:40pm – no but even at 3:30 amidst the rush of high schoolers clumped five six around computers wanting to check *Dude look at this picture Annas posted (to Friendly Social Online Network)* and *So I heard there's this site where they have the whole series for free downloads with like no copyright,* and what kind of high schooler has no choice after school but the children's section of the city library, and why don't you feel worse about their lack of opportunity than you do about a little noise in the children's section? but then what *'civilized'* person could blame you – able, miraculously, at such times to conjure up a smile as pure as on her Cotillion Day. Kate or Elizabeth or some Austen-heroine name, *not* 'Katie' or 'Liz' or, my god, 'Ashlee' or retro-cool 'Matilda' whatever, but something a little more up-do, y'know? Something with a little something held in reserve.

No one knows it but they're the ones hold the whole church together. Of shared joy in knowing. Cold air twined around stone pillars, sunlight in solid beams through beautiful old windows losing slowly their colour, a gather of hopeful faces each day like Christmas: cathedral of learning and of forgiveness, paradise of long-ago innocence regained page by page (I like Frances the Badger and never dug the Berenstain Bears but Kate likes Arthur and Elizabeth dearly loves *The Secret Garden* as you'd well hope). None of it standing even still if it weren't for these three women, each in their late 20s early 30s thereabouts, each loves loving kids, each radiates a serene acceptance that you can't help (looking at them there at the Can We Help You desk beaming at the 3-year-olds who've never seen gerbils before) defiling with the usual projections and impingements: nah not librarian-sex fantasies, my god *cliché,* but cod-psych stuff. Bet she argues all the time with her mom, and knits. Bet she's offended by dirty jokes. Bet she went to an all-girls school and secretly was always super good at math but lost that edge slowly, slowly; and a guy was involved, whom she referred to as a 'boy' even at 25, and blah blah blah. Pathetic really. Then again but *also* sex fantasies of course, because librarians…

And they are good and kind, and hold the church together, and you feel at any moment like you might, just, oh, explode, or *die* because you deserve to. For defiling, deserve to. You know Kate would lift your body gently and toss it into the machine that makes the gerbil food, smiling, and raise your son as her own, brilliant, quiet, maybe scared of some things, certain of others. And he'd have so so many picture books, the books he's always wanted, finally. Secretly you didn't think you knew how to teach him how to read and now you won't have to, it should be a relief, this is hell, RIP.

And –

And but if you have no worlds at all.

No safeworld on the tip of your tongue.

If –

If you're alone in dark. Or it is in you.

If not a single world in the whole word is for you. I mean: what if it's not enough. Or really I mean: what happens *when* you run out of that energy or will-to-freedom or just sense of self. In dark, dark, dark, dazzling dark. Exhausting and immense. Its bulk upon your body cold and too present, too real, and dreaming air can't blow breath onto and throughout you. Daunting.

When escape is impossible and rescue is impossible and forgiveness and transformation are impossible and not just the moment but the place and the whole idea of you become means of oppression. If the blade of you turns upon yourself. And your insides open utterly up and there's nothing to find inside but you dig dig dig into a darkling place and the pricks of light aren't stars, they're, oh god –

Then?

Then what good is a world?

If you can't let go then how did you make it so far from yourself.

♥ ☞ ♣ ☞ ✳

In the beginning was the world. The world was with you. It was you. You gave away the worlding in the word. And the word was without form, or point; and darkness was upon your face. And your pen moved sharp upon the grateful skin of the world yet to be. Its figured face. And you said, let's get something going; and something went. You looked into me, that I was good: and words divided that which becomes into me from those who begin unto you. Up was pretty much down, or wanting was waiting; or I suppose wondering was being. And the evening and the morning were the first day. Letterspills into worlds brand new. Soft music backing the ground. Well look at that. You filled me on up. Lovelymaking of our becoming-body a word. (The world you're thinking of is love, oh my god.)

Then you held my unkissed face like Audubon's bird (the distance between us surprised me, slew me) and said, Let the word be Woven. Let it bind the waters and the waters. Let it blind the Self. Firmly you said it, I remember. Your hand upon my face I called Heaven (or in place of the world that is the name I gave the body that these worlds *mean*). And the evening and the morning were the second day.

But then up comes the sun and it was the last more or less.

And you said, Let it rain. The storm soak us. The very idea of (newly) us bound up in the execution of (covetous) each. The knife stroke. Let it rain! River riot! The ocean weaves, let them rise and reach, cities subversed, beings disordered, I release you, I unwant the sufficiency of you, Jesus Christ *LET IT RAIN* already!

And go on earthquake before us drumming out *We're coming*. Great whales, every live wire every image that moves you, what lives in skin, let them flow into the punctured single cell that was new earth at its conception. The wordbuilding urge, damn! Every winged fowl after her kind, and hereinafter let there be no illusory Good. Us and warm water, that's all.

We kissed, and tasted the same. God it was good.

Fill the waters in the seas. Lie down if you want, if you like. Something new. Or erupt write there standing straight and skyward tall. Birdsong! Nighttime! Streetlight beams bending backwords to slink around crumbled corners, let the skin be scoured *let it rain*. The book of the word. Tens of thousands of worlds arrayed block nightlit by livening block. The city of us. Body our body the word of us is a body and we belong for a greater being. (The world known to all men is *love*, oh my god.)

And the evening and the morning were the third day. The last at last.

       you feel like home

Afterworld

> nobody is truly sane until he feels
> gratitude to the whole universe
>
> Oscar Ichazo

These stories were written together to form this Book – a self-contained (and -containing) world.

The recurring images here – water, weave, world, word, selves dissolving, love devouring, minds, cells, dreams, and above all *bodies* of all sorts – are all part of a web of linked concepts which have been constituting (and troubling) my write-thinking for a while now. My hope is that the *Catalogue* can make of them, and of me, a world for you to live in a while.

These have changed me lately:

- **Zen and the Brain** (James H. Austin MD)
- **Angels in America** (Tony Kushner)
- **'7'** (Prince)
- **The Marriage of Heaven and Hell** (Wm. Blake)
- **The Book of the Damned** (Charles Fort)
- **A General Theory of Love** (Lewis, Amini, Lannon)
- **The Hitchhiker's Guide to the Galaxy** (DNA)

- **Ways of Worldmaking** (Nelson Goodman)
- **Only Revolutions** (Mark Z. Danielewski)
- **Suppressed Transmission** (Kenneth Hite)
- **The Crying of Lot 49** (Thomas Pynchon)
- **The Deviant Moon Tarot** (Patrick Valenza)
- **The Book of Thoth** (Aleister Crowley)
- **Gödel, Escher, Bach** (Douglas Hofstadter)
- **Aegypt** and **Little, Big** (John Crowley)

With the exception of *Ways of Worldmaking* and the two brain books (*Zen* and *General Theory*) I think of these texts as occupying a shared imaginary universe. The heavenly city Prince sings about is the same one Belize describes in *Angels*; Blake's tyger and Valenza's steam-powered chimeras stalk its streets. The omni-mythic America of *Only Revolutions* (watched over by Kushner's angels) expires in Pynchon's NoCal on its west coast and Valenza's Long Island in the east, while rotating around an axis running through Ken Hite's haunted Chicago. Charles Fort is this innerworld's rebel epistemologist, Douglas Adams its satiric conscience, Hofstadter its chief translator, the magus-goof Aleister Crowley its Fool.

Reading one of these texts I hear all the others talking back to it.

Though I try, I can't fit John Crowley's books into this universe; it's possible they created it, or trumped it. His novel *Little, Big* provides *Allworlds'* epigraph, including the line, 'It may be that what we have here isn't a story or an interior, but a Geography'; if this book has a Theory, or (more obviously) an Excuse, that's surely it.

THANKS

I am grateful to the wonderful children's librarians at the Cambridge Public Library, the hardworking professionals at MIT Medical, and our daycare miracle-workers for their assistance. Thanks, too, to the pushers at Luna Cafe, Atomic Bean Cafe, 1369 Coffeehouse, and the big Starbucks in Harvard Square. (What's up Tina!) Thanks also to the Boston Writers' Meetup.

This book wouldn't exist without the following people (in no particular order): Shervin, Norah, ARRRRR, Jeff, Lindsey, The Good Doc, Elissa M Snobbins, the Boston Writer's Meetup, Walter Holland Sr., Phillippe, Cameo, Maciej, Greg and Anna Stachowiak, Walter Biggins, SEK, Thorburn, Milch, and the readers of *blog.waxbanks.net*.

Last and first, to my wife Agi and my son Feliks: Thank you so much. This book is yours as I am, always.

WALLY HOLLAND
CAMBRIDGE MA
OCTOBER 2012

Walter Holland was born in San Juan, grew up near Houston and then near Buffalo, and now lives in Cambridge. He has written several other books (available wherever you got this one), including *A Tiny Space to Move and Breathe*; *Falsehoods, Concerns*; and *Fixing You*.

Walter can be found online at *blog.waxbanks.net*.

Made in the USA
Lexington, KY
26 April 2013